.38 Tales

By Justin White

For my daughter Ellekah, who is my reason for being and for my dearest Elizabeth, who changed my life irrevocably.

1. I Don't Smoke

I turn the collar up my coat and pull the brim of my cap down low. It's a cold night, colder than it should be this time of year. The streets are empty and silent as I make my way down to the corner store. The rain had stopped half an hour before, but the wind, cold and biting still bulled its way through me. Winter's coming early, and she's coming angry. I wrap the coat around me a little tighter; it helps a little but not much.

It wasn't a long walk to the liquor store, but by the time I arrived I had already begun to regret it. The fat little man behind the counter greets me with the same over happy grin he seems to perpetually wear. I didn't think they made people that friendly in this town. He makes my dollar sale feel like he won the jackpot. I can't deal with that much chipper right now.

He slides me the pack of Luckies with a nod and grin. I wave my thanks and make my way back into the night. The first drag feels like heaven, it had been far too long and on a night like this a fine smoke was better than a thick steak and a bottle of cold brew. I jam the pack into the inside pocket of my coat, near to my heart where they belong. I bury my hands in the pockets of my coat and begin the return journey to my hole of an apartment.

The Lucky sat clenched in my lips as I breathe in its sweet, smoky flavor. It made the cold bite harder, it made the walk feel longer, but it had been too many months and I had quit for every wrong reason.

"Hey pal, can I get one of those?" The voice came from behind me. I turn slow and casual, angry for spending too much time daydreaming and not paying enough attention to the world around me. The cold was making me careless.

"Scuse me?" I asked, around the smoke, still gripped tightly in my mouth.

"I said gimme a cigarette pal!" I could smell the stink on him from five paces off, acrid and rank, the ripe aroma of cheap whiskey and vomit. He wasn't the dirty ruin I'd expected to be on the streets this time of night, but he wasn't far from it. This neighborhood always had its share of detritus once the sun went down.

"Yeah, man, why don't you give us all one." I wasn't surprised by the arrival of his two friends; I could hear their heavy footfalls moving in from the alley to my left. It was close to last call, and I'm willing to bet these three had spent all night in the local watering hole. "You look like you could spare a few."

He wasn't wrong. The coat may have been a few years old, but it had cost a lot of money once, same with the hat perched on my head. She always told me I was the only man she ever knew who could dress himself in the morning. She loved that about me.

"Sorry boys, I don't smoke." I said, as I exhaled a large cloud of the poison kiss my lungs craved one second and berated me for the next.

"Oh, he don't smoke!" The first one says. He was the small and angry type, mad the world for shorting him a few inches off the top. "You think that's funny? You some kind of comedian?"

"Naw" I answer. "I quit a year ago." I let the butt fall from my lips and crush the embers beneath my heel. "It'll kill ya, you know."

"How's about we just take your wallet then funny man?"

I lean back as something whizzes by my head. One of thugs from the alley had a pipe, and had he been a little more sober he would have mashed in the side of my skull. I stick a foot out and send him tumbling into the gutter, rainwater spraying as he collapses face first into the street.

"You boys need to call it a night. Go sleep it off and no hard feelings on my part." My hands are still my pockets, no need to make this uglier.

"Fuck your hard feelings man!" The little man is reaching into his waistband, and I knew this would only get worse. I step into the little man as he fumbles for the gun I know he's reaching for. His friend from the alley makes his move; I hear the leather tear on the back of my coat as his stumbling swipe went wide.

I kick hard and feel a satisfying crunch as shoe meets knee. He screams as he goes down, clutching at his useless leg. Shorty had finally pulled his piece free, but I was already on top of him. I seized his gun hand, guiding it down and away from my torso.

He fires, then again! The racket made my ears ring like the devil but I held firm, forcing the pistol away from me. My right hand came free of my pocket, the switchblade out and glinting in the streetlight. I rammed it home in his throat, once, twice, a third time! His knees buckle and he collapses to the sidewalk. The gun clatters to the wet cement as he clutches his throat, desperately fighting to hold in his life's blood. It wasn't long before he stopped squirming.

It was only then I notice broken knee has stopped shouting, one of the errant shots had taken the top of his skull clean off. I don't envy the poor bastard that has to clean this mess up. The one with the pipe was long gone; I doubt I'll see his face again. I pull the pack of Luckys from my coat, and light up, taking a long inhale. My coat is ruined; bastard ripped it near in half. I drop it on the leftover meat on the sidewalk.

I'm going to miss that coat.

2. Somebody

The problem with having been somebody once, is that the people who you want to remember never do, and the ones you wish to hell would forget never will. It had been six months since Jack stopped taking my calls.

I sit in my little corner of the Deuce of Clubs, savoring the dollar beer and the heavy, smoke filled air. It's busy for a Wednesday night, the chill outside has chased in a few fresh faces. The small stage in the corner is cluttered with the remains of tonight's live entertainment, a blues trio no one ever heard of and god-willing never will again. The beer is warmer than it ought to be and tastes like what they must serve in Hades. I raise my empty glass to catch Franklin's eye.

"Nuther one boss?" he shouts from across the room, his rich baritone cutting through the din of the regulars making their small talk.

"Yeah, thanks." I'm not sure he hears me, but he sends the bar girl round with a fresh glass. She gives me a smile and a wink.

"This one's on me, sugar." I nod my thanks, having already forgotten her name. I should be ashamed of myself. The front man for what passed as tonight's entertainment makes his way across the room and plants himself in the booth opposite to me. His suit is cheap, the navy blue had faded to more of a garish light purple. I'm not certain he thinks twice about how ridiculous he looks, or if maybe that's part of the act.

"I know I seen you someplace before." His voice is like gravel under tires, it grates on my nerves and after an hour of his alleged singing I am more than willing to give up the chance to hear more of it.

"Sorry friend, don't think we've met before." I flip open the battered silver Zippo and light up. I'm hoping he'll take my meaning.

"Naw, naw! I saw you at The Palace, must have been going on five years ago now. I know it was you!"

"You must be thinking of somebody else, friend." I blow out a large could of smoke, obscuring his face for a moment. Sadly, he's still there as the cloud fades away.

"Come on buddy, have a drink with me an' the boys, it'd mean a lot to 'em."

"I'm sorry friend, I like my spot here just fine and I'm not in much of a mood to chat. Thanks for the trip down memory lane." I take a long pull off my brew and settle back into my booth. "Have yourself a fine evening."

"Oh, so you Mr Bigtime huh? Or you to good to come drink with a few brothers? Man, fuck you, you Honkey piece of shit!" He up now and angry, fists balled and teeth clenched.

"It ain't like that buddy, it ain't like that at all." I've seen his type a thousand times in my life, mad at everybody because he's still nobody. Mad at anyone who was ever anything, while he toils away at being nothing. "Look friend, let me get you beer and we can all have a nice night huh?"

"I ain't yo friend cracker! Get yo white ass up!" He's seeing red now.

"Hey, it's time fo' you boys to go. You played yo set, and you gots yo pay all nice and square. Pick up yo gear and git." Franklin's involved now. I feel like hell causing trouble in his joint, hard enough times as it is.

"Listen you busted up one legged old fool, shut yo damn mouth! Why you gotta serve this Honkey fuck and tell us to git! I oughtta come back there and give you a piece of what he's about to get, you old Uncle Tom mother fucker!" I'm on my feet now, blood pounding in my ears, I'm ready to punch this prick's nose though the back of his head when I hear it, the slow chick-chack of a shotgun being pumped.

"I done tol you once already. Get yo shit, and get out of my bar." He holds the twelve gauge leveled at the gravel mouthed young buck. His two buddies look at him, wide eyed with horror and for one second I think he's about to do something monumentally stupid. He waves his hand dismissively at Franklin.

"Man, fuck this place! Come on boys, get yo shit. Fuck all these dumb ass mother fuckers!" He and his boys pack up quick and hustle to the door. He takes the time to shoot me one last, angry look before the door slams and I hear the squeal of tires in the parking lot. Part of me prays they hit a light post. As the sound of the engines fades down the street I know one more prayer is going unanswered.

"Sorry about all that, Franklin." I say as I plant myself back in my little corner. The shocked silence fades, the regulars have seen this show before, no one even moved for the exit. Life quickly returns to normal and the place becomes abuzz with conversation again.

"Ain't no big deal. You want another boss?" He holds up a fresh glass of his piss-water beer.

"Yeah, thanks."

3. Bad News

Jimmy Knuckles slides himself smoothly into the booth opposite me. His dark pin-stripe suit is immaculately pressed and one of the finest I've ever seen. I've heard that he never wears the same suit twice in a month; I'm not sure he wears the same one twice at all. He glowers at the patronage of the ironically named little café, scanning the room before he begins to speak.

"Uncle Vito has asked me to deliver this to you." He reaches into his coat and I'm not ashamed to say I catch myself flinching as he pulls out a small envelope. He spills out the contents on the table, and slides them over to me. One is 5x7 photograph of a man wearing sunglasses and a long overcoat, his light hair is slicked back, a cigar hangs from his lips. "This man knows what you wish to know. This man has your answer."

My stomach churns as my eyes burn in a hole in the picture. My plate of ham and eggs is totally forgotten as I pick it up off the uneven faux wood table. I remember this face. For a moment I forget who it is sitting at my table, until he clears his throat. Jimmy holds up the second item.

"This is an invitation to my Uncle's club. You are to join him for dinner tonight at precisely 7 o'clock. I am to offer you this one caveat however. If you should appear as invited, and if Don Candolini should provide you the name of the individual herein pictured, your acquaintanceship is forthwith terminated."

That wasn't a big surprise, I knew what I was asking when I went to the Old Man for a favor. Jimmy sits anxiously, glaring at me, waiting for a response. I know he wants me to say yes, and I know he's hated me from day one. I'm alright with that.

"Please tell Don Candolini I'll be there promptly, Mr.

Nocilioni." Jimmy nods and grins his foul grin. I'm not sure what I did to grind his gears so bad, or if maybe it just burns him that his uncle Vito likes me so much. Whatever it is, it won't matter after tonight. He gets up and without a word or a backwards glance he's gone. I haven't let go of the photograph, my memory burns with this face. I know I'll see him again soon. I pay my bill and leave my half eaten plate on the table along with a five dollar tip.

It's raining outside, a cold stinging rain that feels like a thousand little needles jabbing my face. I welcome it. I open my arms and let it take a bite out of me. The cold feels good, it feels right. I make my way home with a look on my face that makes people stand aside as I pass. I'm soaked to the skin by the time I get to my apartment, but I don't care, not one lick. I've got all day to spend, and it can't pass quick enough.

At 6:30 I'm showered and shaved and on the way to Vito's. I'm in my finest suit, which still makes me stick out like a sore thumb among the city's high rollers. There's already a line out front by the time I arrive. I pass by ladies with fur coats and handmade Italian shoes. I pass men who could buy and sell a thousand souls a thousand times over and not even notice they'd spent the change to do it. I approach the gorilla in the finely made monkey suit at the door. He's a new face, young and massive and eager to hand me my head.

"Line's back there mac." He gestures with his thumb to the back of the line. "So blow!" I reach into my coat, slowly, no need to spook the big ape, and produce the hand signed invitation from the Old Man himself. I hold it up high and close to his face so he gets a good clean look at it. His eyes go wide as dinner plates as he moves the velvet rope aside. "S..sorry sir! Mr. Candolini is waiting for you at his usual table sir!"

He sighs in relief as I walk past without another word, all too conscious of the mistake he almost made. There was a reason the old man was called "The Shark" and the quickest way to find out why was to interfere with his business. The band is just starting up as I make my way inside, they're pretty solid, but I'd expect no less. The room is fragrant with the sweet aromas of fine tobacco and expensive perfumes from all over the world. One of the Don's soldiers spots me and waves me over to his table.

Don Vito "The Shark" Candolini, stands to greet me. His weathered features and stark white hair are a luxury for a man in his business. He's lived to a ripe old age by being smarter and more ruthless than anyone I've ever met. He hugs me, and motions for me to sit across his table from him. A plate of tortellini is already out and waiting for me.

"Sit, sit. Let's have a nice dinner before we talk business, huh?" The Don's voice is as coarse and raspy as a sandpaper shirt. "I had Gino make up your favorite." I thank him and we sit down to eat. The food is divine, but Don Candolini would tolerate no less. We wash it down with a bottle of wine that's older than I am, and he offers me a hand rolled Cuban cigar. I don't refuse.

"Ey, Anotnio, get the fuck outta here so my friend and I can talk, huh!" The goon standing guard nods his head and makes himself scarce. I'm flattered, I can count on one hand the number of times Vito's been left alone in the last twenty years. He takes a folded piece of paper out of his coat and tosses it on the table in front of me. I reach for it, but he stops me.

"I gotta tell you son, before you open that, this is bad news. You do what I think you gonna do and I can't help you. I can't protect you from what comes next. You're a good kid, and I don't wanna see you get yourself dead."

"I don't think Jimmy would mind too much." I blow a sorry smoke ring; it hovers for a moment then fades into nothing. The Cuban tastes like heaven.

"Ah Jimmy. All that book learning, all his big words and he don't have the sense God gave a donkey! It breaks my heart to know all this is gonna be his one day. He don't know who is friends are. Do me a favor huh? Don't open that here. Soon as you do, we're done. Soon as you do you there ain't no more you and me. All the years you never ask for one thing, and then you gotta go and do this to me."

"Sorry, Vito. You know how it is sometimes." I put the paper in my coat. We both stand and embrace again.

"Yeah, I know. God knows I know. It was nice having you here son, don't go get yourself dead, huh?"

"Thank you Vito, give Adriana my love?" He nods and waves me off. I make my way to the door, paper still folded in my pocket. I step out of Vito's for the last time and into the frigid night. I unfold the thin sheet and read the two words I've been hunting for since it all went to hell, Tommy Monaghan.

4. The Virtue of Patience

My .38 is out and in my hand, he has a hundred bullets, I've got six.

Bits of masonry rain down on my head as the low brick wall is chopped to ruins. .45 slugs burn through the chilly night, shredding the still silence and wrecking any hopes I had of making this clean. Of course this wasn't going to go down easy, what the hell was I thinking. Smoke pours from the barrel of the sub machine gun, as Tommy "Gun" Monaghan, takes cover behind his Packard. It's sleek and black and brand new, it seems someone had dropped a Molotov cocktail on his previous ride.

"So, tough guy, you wanted to see me? Well here I am!" He pops up again, pouring white hot death in buckets down on my feeble shelter. I crawl on my belly, face down in the wet grass and fragrant earth of some unlucky bastard's front lawn. The lights inside are still dark and I hope to hell no one's home. Tommy's getting sloppy, and I know I've made him mad.

He's still busy mangling the wall by the time I've low crawled around it and rolled into the street. I crouch down behind a beat up old Ford and bide my time. The Tommy Gun clicks, the devil roar subsides. I'm about to make my move when he drops the massive ammo drum and slams home a new one. He's locked and loaded quick as lightning and I roll back into cover.

"Don't tell me yer dead already tough guy? Me an you, we got a long evening ahead!" He shouts into the night. I'm still as the grave as he pops up, sprays a burst of lead poison and is up and over the wall in a flash. He's good, a killer born, fast and skilled, but he's spitting mad at the hell I've made life for him and his boys in the past few weeks. He's not thinking straight, or he wouldn't have come alone.

It doesn't take him long to find the trail I've left through the soft earth and grass. Glass shatters and the shards drift down in a jagged, deadly rain. They look beautiful in the dim yellow streetlights. He hoses down the old Ford and its sheer dumb luck I don't catch a slug for my troubles. He's laughing at me now, punctuating his insane guffaws with bursts from the Thompson.

"Come on out tough guy! We can do this fast or slow, I got all night!" He squeezes the trigger and the leaden storm begins again. I hear the Thompson go "click" but I'm ready this time. I'm up; the revolver barks twice, barely a whimper after the deafening roar of the Tommy Gun. The first shot takes him high on the right shoulder, the second crashes into his left knee sending him down in a heap of broken bones and bleeding agony.

I light up a Lucky as I casually stroll over to where Tommy lies. He's trying like mad to make his arm work, to ram home another drum of .45's but his right arm just flops next to him, limp and useless. I kick the Tommy Gun out of his left hand into the street and stomp down hard. I feel fingers snap. He screams as I lean in close and look over the wounds on his arm and leg.

"That's nasty Tommy boy. I think you might need a Doctor." I can see the spare ammo drums under his coat; he came loaded for a war. All that for little old me, I'm deeply touched. His eyes are fearful, but he still plays the dangerous man.

"You're gonna need a coroner! You know who I am, tough guy, huh? You know who the fuck I am!?!" His voice is a shriek, pleading and shrill. He's panicking bad, the shock and blood loss are seizing control.

"Yeah Tommy, I do. Tommy 'Gun' Monaghan. Killer, thug, all around son of a bitch. You're also the bleeding sack of feces who is going to die right here in the street like a dog." I take a drag of the Lucky and exhale a cloud in his face. "Now, you're going to tell me a story Tommy, and you're going to make it a good one." He does.

One last shot rings out in the silence of the night. I think long and hard about taking the Thompson with me, he won't need it anymore after all. In the end I leave it where it lay. Toys like that make you sloppy; make you forget the virtue of patience. It's all too easy to charge in spraying hot death and catch one right in the back for your trouble. Time's on my side now. I whistle to myself as I duck down the next street. Time is on my side.

5. Days like These

"Raise" I say, tossing two more chips into the already substantial pot. Billy chomps on the end of his cigar, mulling over his hand. Franky and Pete have already folded.

"Raise!" He grumbles at me, adding four more chips to the mountain at the center of the table. Billy never bluffs, he knows he has the worst poker face in three counties, but he is God damn lucky.

"All in." I push my stack of chips into the middle of the table. I know Billy can't match it. He fumbles for a moment at the heaping pile of money. Laying his cards face down he pulls out his wallet and tosses something on the pile.

"My ticket to the fights tonight, good enough?" I nod. "Call." He lays down his cards and chuckles, his jowly, stubbly face bobbing up and down. "Four deuces, thanks for the payday buddy!" He spreads his arms wide to rake in his winnings. I put a hand on his wrist.

"Might want to wait a moment, Bill." I lay my hand down, straight flush, eight high.

"You dirty…." Bill starts while Franky and Pete bust up laughing. I rake the mountain of chips into my hat and slip the ticket into my front pocket.

"If you'll excuse me boys, don't wanna be late." Billy hits me with a stream of vitriol that would make a drill sergeant blush. He's still cursing my name by the time I cash out and hit the door. Fifty dollars richer and with the prospect of watching "Irish" Jack O'Malley demolish some poor palooka ahead of me I strut the five blocks downtown.

It looks like Christmas at the sports arena, this city may not be much, but she loves her native sons. Jack's name is up in lights, twice as large as the poor chump who's his next stop on the road to the belt. I make my way inside, following the herd of people and find my seat. Tenth row, Billy really went all out tonight. I flag down the beer vendor and have him send one my way then settle in to enjoy the under card.

I'm five rounds into Has Been V. Never Was when I see them. The greenest, most perfect eyes I've ever seen, looking back at me from two rows up. It takes me a moment to notice the rest of her but when I do she makes my heart stop. She's standing now, making her way out to the aisle, and I get an eyeful. Tall and curvaceous, with those perfect emerald orbs shining out underneath a mane of raven dark hair, I know I can't resist. She smiles at me, a smile full of promise. I'm out of my seat and following her down the aisle before I have time to think. What the hell is wrong with me?

She leads me into the back, away from the cheering masses and the crush of humanity. I can hear the crowd roaring as she grabs me by the tie and pulls me in for a fierce, passionate kiss. I know it's not me they're roaring for, but it sure as hell feels like it.

"Come on" she whispers in my ear. She turns and drags her porcelain hand slowly down my tie pulling it gently until she reaches the end and it flops down against my chest. I follow, to eager and to entranced by the swaying of her hips in her tight black dress to notice where she's led me. She turns and pulls me in again, her lips locking on to mine with hunger I've never felt before. She pulls herself away and gives me that smile again. Times like this, I forget I'm the unluckiest bastard on Earth.

Stars explode behind my eyes as something hard and cold collides with the back of my skull. I drop like a Lead balloon, collapsing at her feet. I'm not quite out, but might as well be. She always told me I had a thick skull.

"This the guy?" I hear the siren's voice from someplace far off.

"Aye, tis he. Thank you Delilah dear."

"Sorry, handsome, nothing personal." She whispers in my ear before the click clack of her heels fades down the concrete hallway. My sense are coming back to me a little, voices don't sounds like their coming through ten fathoms of water now.

"Still awake there tough guy?" I feel a wingtip explode into my ribs. White hot fire shoots through my chest and I'm sure something snapped. I let out a groan as I curl up to protect myself. Another boot to the back of my head and I'm seeing black. "This ain't yer' lucky day pal." I hear the click of a hammer being cocked and I know I'm done. They suckered me and I walked right into it like a cow at the rendering plant outside of town. I close my eyes and wait for the world to explode.

I hear my mystery assailant gasp and hear the thud as he collapses next to me. I feel rough hands grab me and haul me to my feet.

"Get the fuck up ya daft idiot." My vision clears and I'm face to face with biggest Irishman I've ever seen. "Irish" Jack O'Malley may have been born in America, but he sounds fresh out of a Dublin slum. "What in the name Mary Mother o' God are you up to?"

"Jack, been a while." I manage, rubbing the massive lumps forming on the back of head. I try to breathe slow and easy, the fire in my side subsiding. "Seems to have been a bit of a misunderstanding. Sorry, I'll take care of it."

"Ah no need for that, now. I'll have the boys see to him in a minute. You look like shit, boyo. Why don't you pop on home and have a rest." Arguing with Jack was never a winning proposition, so I nod my pounding head slowly.

"Yeah, I'll catch the fight on the radio." I pick up my battered hat and turn to go "Thanks." I say over my shoulder.

"Aw, think nothing of it." I start to make my way to a rear exit, no point in getting seen by anyone else tonight.

"Hey!" Jack shouts. I stop and turn to face him. "Why don't ya come round for supper this week? Maggie'd be glad to see ya."

"Sure Jack, thanks." He waves his massive right hand as I slip out the back. A chain gang hammers in my head as I make my way home. My side hurts like the devil, but I'm still alive. Days like these, that's all I can ask.

6. Better than You

"I need a favor." I place my gloved hands on the heavy bag I've been working and stop it mid swing.

"No."

"Ya didn't even ask what it is yet!" The old man waves his arms at me in exasperation. "I just need ya ta…"

"Not interested." I lift my fists and get ready to go back to work, when Kelly steps between me and the bag. I'm just here to work out some kinks; I'm not looking to do any favors today.

"Killer" Kelly McBride, ex middleweight champ and owners of McBride's Gym does not budge. His red hair has gone as grey as his eyes, but he still has the assassin's stare. He raises one bony fist, knuckles swollen with arthritis and too many years of bashing in skulls.

"Why you're as bad as the rest o' these young punks! No respect for anybody. I ought to give ya one o' these here and learn ya a thing or two about pain!" I relent, I like the old codger. He's been a good friend in ugly days.

"Ok, what do you need?"

"Ah, that's ma boy! I knew I could count on you! I got dis young gun over dere who seems to think he knows everything about foightin' God ever put on dis here Earth. I need ya ta go knock him down a peg, maybe teach him a bit o' humility." I glance over to the ring in the center of the Gym. I get a good look at the young gun and start to regret opening my mouth. He's massive, with muscles like corded steel cables and fists the size of Easter hams. He moves and dances around the ring, shadow boxing, fists cutting through the air in a blur.

"Fifty bucks." I say, without a hint of sarcasm.

"Fifty!" Kelly splutters and curses "Oh no! I'll go twenty foive and no higher, ya rogue!"

"Thirty five and I get two months dues free."

"You're a thief and a villain! Its highway robbery is what it is! Thirty and one month, and that's all! Takin' an' old man's money!" I smile and offer my hand. He shakes it with his arthritic paw. "You're a good egg sonny jim! Now go give dat fella a lesson in respect!"

I dig my mouth guard out of my bag and make my way to ring. He notices me as I'm climbing through the ropes.

"Who the hell are you supposed to be?" he asks with a sneer.

"I'm today's instructor. Kelly said you needed some work." He laughs; he must have forty pounds and fifteen years on me. He's one of those neckless monstrosities you see in nightmares. He's David come to life with a shaved head and a sneer. "Get your gloves on."

"I'll take it easy on you pop, don't worry." He waves over one of the trainers to tie on his gloves and put in his mouth piece. Kelly waits till he's ready and rings the bell. I put my fists up and advance, slow and methodical. He's not taking me seriously. The young gun dances and clowns, his hands down by his waist. Activity stops in the gym as the patrons gather round. He's humiliated more than a few of these boys.

I snap out two quick jabs and wipe the smirk right off his face. A left cross crashes into his eye and he's taking me seriously now. I catch a left on the gloves and it pushes me a half step back. I duck under a right hook and land a counter to his ribs. It feels like punching concrete. He shoves me back with both hands and takes a wild swing at my head. I block is partially but my ear begins to ring. He's strong, too strong.

I advance again, ducking a combination that would have knocked me flat. I come up with a right hook that catches him clean in the eye, and then I follow it up with a left uppercut that snaps his head back. He takes half step backwards, gloves coming up to cover his face but I stay on him I land two hard rights to his ribs. My hand throbs inside the glove, but I can tell he's feeling it now. He tries to shove me away again, but I weave aside and shove him along with my left arm. He stagers to the middle of the ring, he spins to face me and is greeted with an overhand right that shuts his left eye.

He lashes out with a left that clips my chin and snaps my head to the side; it feels like I caught a bowling ball with my teeth. A monster left come whistling in, but I get my gloves up in time, my arms shuddering with the impact! He's got his balance back and is on the attack now firing rights and lefts! I bob and weave, knocking the blows aside and looking for my opening. He swings from his shoes, a savage right haymaker meant to end the fight in one punch. It's all I need.

I slip the punch, dodging past it and retuning fire, crashing another right hook down into his exposed eye! He stagers to the side and I stand him up with a left uppercut to the chin, he takes two steps backwards and crashes to the mat. Kelly rings the bell and the crowd gives me a cheer! They're already clapping me on the back as I step back out through the ropes. Kelly's got the smelling salts and is slapping the young gun awake.

"Get up ya great heap. See dat dere, dat's how ya foight a man. No matter how good ya think ya are, dere's someone in the world better'n you! Remember dat next time ya smart off!"

God damn my jaw hurts.

7. The Way Life Works

It's amazing how easy it is to hide in plain sight. A handful of Palmade and motorcycle jacket and I'm one more piece of greaser street trash. I've been shadowing the Riordan brothers for three blocks and they haven't even looked my way. I'm just one more little fish in their big pond, too small to be worthy of their attention. It's the middle of the day, but the street is nearly abandoned. People know better.

Blake and Billy Riordan make their way into each business on this little road. Twin bald heads and twin handlebar mustaches bob blithely down the way, in and out, in and out. They don't stay in quite long enough to make a purchase, and I don't see any parcels. It's collection day. It's broad daylight and no one says a word, no one calls the cops, no one even dares to look at them as they help themselves to the life's blood of everyone in the neighborhood. Twin kings striding though their tiny kingdom, once a week Gods making the mortals suffer for their pleasure. I've watched them make their rounds three times now. Every week it's the same story, and I've seen it often enough.

I follow them to the end of the street, watching them rob every mom & pop shop they pass. It makes me ill, and it makes me angry. I hear them laugh and joke, the sound of it grates in my ears like nails down a chalkboard. They duck into the same side alley, on their way to someplace honest men would never go. I flip a smoke between my lips and make my move. I'm on them before they can react.

"Hey buddy, can I bum a light?"

"What the f.." Billy starts, the words turning into a gurgle as I bury my switchblade to the hilt in his neck. I see a flicker of recognition before his eyes go dark, he knows who it is who killed him. I pull my piece as Billy's leaking corpse flops over, my knife still jutting from the wound. I point the .38 right between Blake's eyes and he freezes. Easy living rolling sheep for their nickels has made him soft and slow.

"What's a matter Blake? Didn't expect to see me so soon?"

"Oh God! Oh no, please!" He goes from frozen in terror to shaking like the last leaf in the autumn wind. His eyes well up with tears and I'm even more disgusted with him. "Please, take the money, take all of it! Oh God!"

"Stop shaking you damn coward!" It's all I can do not to pull the trigger and put him out of his misery. "You're going to take a message to Danny Doyle for me. You tell him I'm coming for him, him and every damn member of his mob that was there, you know the night. You tell the whole God damn gang that I don't care about the rest of them, ten names, ten men, that's all I'm after. Better make that eight now, what with Tommy's sudden demise and your brother's tragic passing." I seize him by the collar and drag his face an inch from mine. "Are we clear?" I snarl, my eyes filled with hate.

"O…okay! I'll tell him! I'll tell him!" I shove the quivering mass to the street. I'm sick to my stomach, sick at what we've both become. I can't help but shake my head as I turn to go. I haven't taken two steps before I turn and fire, the slug catching him between the eyes and making an awful mess of the pavement behind him. A snub nosed revolver clatters to the pavement, dropping from nerveless fingers. I really wish he hadn't done that.

I search both men, finding two wallets full of hundreds and twenty five envelopes stuffed with greenbacks. I help myself to the contents of their wallets; I figure that's mine fair and square. I gather up the envelopes and retrieve my switchblade, wiping it off on Billy's coat before I pocket it again. It's a good knife, the best I've ever owned, and it'd be a shame to let it rust in a piece of filth like

Billy Riordan. I spend the rest of my afternoon going door to door, returning the envelopes. They stare at me, some in awe, and some in horror. Not one of the sheep knows what to make of me.

No one thanks me, no one says a word to me, and no one calls the cops. I wanted to send a message; this will have to do. I walk home, enjoying the feeling of the sun on my face for the first time in weeks. The sunshine never lasts in this town, there's always another storm lurking off the coast, waiting for its turn to purge the streets of the meek and mild. You learn to live with it; it's the way life works.

8. If You Could See Me Now

I fumble with the key, finally finding the lock. The wind is whipping a frozen knife through the night; it's not helping me at all. My vision is blurry and my hands are shaking but I manage to get the door open. I don't bother with the light. I can't recall if I remembered to lock the door as I collapse fully clothed into bed, rumpling my already rumpled suit and crushing my hat. My head spins and swirls, sucking me down into unconsciousness.

The dream comes again, as it always does. I'm there in the horrible moment my world turned to ash. I'm helpless, bleeding on the floor as everything beautiful in my life dies again and again and again. The sun is already well into the sky by the time I fight my way back into the waking world. A beam of light smacks me right across the eyes and I can't help but recoil. I drag myself out of bed, unsteady on my feet. I stagger through the mounds of unwashed clothing and empty Chinese take-out and into the bathroom.

I get a good look at myself in the mirror as I undress, I wish I hadn't. My right eye is swollen and black; my knuckles are split and cracked. The massive, ugly scar on my chest is white and dead and cold. I can still feel the burn of the bullet as it tore me open, I can still see the horror in your eyes. If you could see me now, if you could see what I've become, I know it'd break your heart. I tear myself from the mirror and the memories of a life that's no longer mine.

The water is warm and soothes the ache in my muscles. I let it run down my neck and try not to acknowledge how stiff the cold makes me these days. It's been the coldest winter anyone around here can remember and when you're out in that every night, it takes its toll. The water starts to run cold, I've pushed the little water heater as far as it's going to go today. I'm toweling myself off when I notice it, the scent of Jasmine and Honeysuckle, the scent of the siren, Delilah.

"Bang! You're dead, handsome." She steps out of my little kitchen; a beer in one hand, a pearl handled, nickel plated .45 in the other. "You're starting to get careless. You never noticed me tail you back here last night." She shakes her head "It's a little embarrassing."

"I think I was concussed. Little early for the drink."

"It's always afternoon somewhere. Why don't you have a seat."

"Mind if I put on some pants?" She cocks her head to side and gives me a thoughtful look.

"Yes, I do. Have a seat." I shrug and plant myself on the side of the bed. My gun is across the room, hanging in the shoulder holster I wear under my jacket. It might as well be in China. "So, here's my problem. I'm supposed to kill you." She takes a pull off the beer and makes a sour face. "Oh, you really need to invest in some better alcohol."

"Sorry it's not to your liking. I'll be sure to pick up something a little higher class next time I'm out."

"Good! I'm not terribly interested in putting another hole in your chest, so what's a girl to do?" She puts the beer down on what passes for my desk.

"Lure me into the back of the sports arena again and get my head busted open?"

"Oh, that was before I knew you. That doesn't even count." She moves across the room to where my .38 hangs, and pulls it free. She points it right at my chest. "Look at this relic; I'd be embarrassed to be killed by this antique."

"It was a gift."

"Oh yes, yes, fine. Look, Danny Doyle just gave me an enormous sum of money to bring this back to him as proof you're dead. So…I'm going to take a fabulous vacation to Europe."

"How much?"

"Ten large! For you! Can you believe it? You're making him sweat, he's know you're coming for him soon enough. And after what you did to the Riordan brothers…" she lets her voice drop off.

"He's going to kill you for this."

"I'm sure he won't get the opportunity." She slides my pistol back into the holster, slowly and sensually. I feel a shiver run up my spine. She makes her way to the door. "Don't let me down, Slugger. I'll see you in a month or two." With that she's out the door.

The scent still lingers in my ramshackle little dump as I get dressed and head outside. She's long gone. Two weeks later I get a parcel in the post, no return address. I unwrap the plain brown paper to find a beautifully crafted cherry wood case, containing a pair of nickel plated, pearl handled colt 1911s and small card. The note is brief.

Use a Real Gun, D

9. I Hate This Town

I hate this town. I hate what it does to good men. I hate how it breaks your back over its monstrous knee then laughs as you try to crawl away.

There's a sobbing, drunken wreck at my table who used to be Jeremiah Randall. Yes, that Jeremiah Randall, owner of the Randall Auto Works and the richest man in town. This is the fifth night in a row he's been to the Deuce of Clubs and the fifth night he's going home half dead. I can't blame him.

I sit in my little corner; smoking a Lucky and watching him crumble. I don't know what to say to him, and I may be the only man in the world who can genuinely relate. So I sit, and smoke and listen to the first piece of passable entertainment the Deuce has had in months. With all the money Jerry's been throwing around, Franklin could finally afford to pay someone who can play a little.

He looks up, red eyed and bleary and notices his bottle has given up its last drop. He waves to the bargirl.

"He...hey Jenny.....'nother one please." She looks to me and I nod, better he goes under here where I can keep an eye on him. She sashays over and leaves him another bottle of some nameless Kentucky sour mash, Jerry won't notice. He tosses a fifty onto her tray and waves her off. He doesn't even bother with the glass anymore, he just pours down a long belt of what passes for whiskey. The sobs come again and he slumps face first back onto the table, poor bastard.

Jerry Randall went to a war with nothing but a smile on his lips and love of country in his heart, a regular guy just like millions of others. He spent the war fighting from one little island in the pacific to another and he never lost that smile. He came home with a chest full of medals, a movie star wife he met on a two day furlough in San Diego and a will naming him the sole heir of his great uncle Victor Cromwell Randall's estate. He had everything, and then someone took it all away.

The story made all the papers. The entirety of the Randall estate was burned to the ground, the butler's body was found along with two other unidentified corpses. They never found a trace of Samantha. Jerry was half a world away when he got the news. He's been back less than a week and he's spent most of it here. I know how this story ends, and it only gets uglier. He stops sobbing for a moment and takes another deep swig of the hooch.

"Ga-dammit!" He hurls the half empty bottle across the room and it bursts into a thousand little shards, staining the wall with its noxious contents. Franklin motions to the door and I know it's time to get Jerry out of here.

"Come on Jerry, I think you've had enough." He doesn't argue as I help him to his feet. I give Franklin a nod as I walk Jerry out into the night. I half carry half drag him out to his shiny new Ford. He's muttering, crying and completely useless. I jam him into the passenger seat and head uptown to the Metropolitan.

The Met is the best hotel in our little burgh, near the river and with a breathtaking view of the bay from the penthouse. The doorman waves us in; I'm becoming something of a regular here. It's a long ride up the elevator, trying to keep Jerry upright and not puking all over my shoes. He's almost dead unconscious as I steer him to the door to the suite. He's already snoring as I deposit him, fully clothed, onto his bed. I debate for a moment on borrowing his car and heading home, but only for a moment. I help myself to some gin and sack out on the couch, again. The moaning of the damned wakes me from my slumber, and I know a truly monumental hangover is making its presence felt.

"Oh God....."

"Welcome back to the living world." My voice is slightly louder than it has to be. Jerry flinches at every word. "Got yourself thrown out of the Deuce again." He's grabbing his temples and rubbing tenderly.

"I'm sorry….thanks for getting me back home again." I hand him a bottle of aspirin, and he swallows two dry.

"We need to put an end to this, Jerry. If you're going to kill yourself there are faster ways."

"I'm sorry buddy. I feel so damn useless! The cops in this town aren't worth spit! Not one damn lead! Nothing! I swear to Christ I want to find them, I want to find them and make them pay! You know people, right?" His eyes are burning and eager now, anger fighting through the pain. "Talk to Vito for me, help me find them!" I don't know what to say. I want to tell him to let go, to pick up his life and get as far from this hell-hole as he can. I want to tell him to go live and find new love, but I'd be a hypocrite and a liar and I already hate myself enough.

"Jerry, don't ask me that. You don't want this life; you don't want to be what I am. I have too much blood on my hands and there's only more coming. I spend my nights amongst the filth that haunts this miserable city. One by one I am killing every one of those responsible for taking my life from me. I'm a damned monster, Jerry and I can't stop!" I'm roaring now, a lion claiming its kill. I pull my knife and press the switch to pop it open. It shines in the morning sun streaming through the open curtains into the penthouse. "You see this knife, Jerry. Not two weeks ago I stabbed a man to death with this knife. I killed him in the street like a dog then I shot his brother in the face and walked away like it was nothing! Nothing! You're a better, stronger man than I am Jerry. You don't want this life." My rage is spent, and my voice drops to a weary sigh. "You don't want this Jerry…"

Jeremiah Randall is a war hero, a Marine and a proud man,

but I see the fear in his eyes. I pray to God it's enough to keep him on the straight and narrow. I grab my hat and take my leave without another word. Jerry is still sitting, staring at the floor as I shut the door behind me. I don't see him at the Deuce that night. Maybe this once, I got something right.

10. The War Comes Home

The snow is falling gently, it coats our city in a layer or pristine whiteness. By morning it'll be grayish brown slush, trod and trampled, its beauty lost to the world. I'm standing on a rooftop with a fine view of the Club Riviera; the snow blanketing the city is starting to cover me as well. I've been out here for over an hour, watching, waiting, biding my time.

The wind picks up; pushing the snow into my face and making me wish I had a better coat. I can feel the cold steel of the rifle through my gloves; I wipe the lenses of the scope again and peer through. The goon at the door looks just as unhappy as I do. I know he can hear the music and the good cheer inside the club; he's one thin door away from warmth and light and unemployment.

I take my eye away and adjust the scope for the wind; it's coming in just hard enough to alter the shot, blowing in off the sea. I can smell the scents of the harbor and am filled with a strong craving for hot plate of fried Haddock. A fog horn blares, long and low and just loud enough for the breeze to carry it to my ears. It takes me back.

I check the rifle again. The M1903 Springfield is souvenir from my time in the Army. I'm a fluke in this city; like many a harbor town it produced its fair share of Sailors and Marines, I never much cared for boats, so when the call went out I joined the Army and I went to war. I was barely out of Basic before the War Department decided I'd be more valuable parading around the country playing the patriotic son and pitching war bonds from sea to shining sea. I guess that's what you get for doing what I did for a living. I never once fired my rifle in anger.

I check my sight line again; everything is clear and absolutely perfect. The breeze is sharp, but slow, the snow has slowed to only a few random flakes. Now all I need to do is wait and I'm one step closer. Minutes tick off the clock as I sit in the freezing cold. I can feel the stiffness creeping into my bones. I'm into the second hour on the rooftop when I catch my break. "Bully" Blaine Muldoon and the big man himself, Danny Doyle, make their way out the front door. I'm tempted, sorely tempted, to put a bullet through Doyle's heart, but it's not his time. I want him broken and terrified before the end. I want him to lose every night's worth of sleep he's got left in his rapidly shortening life. I want him to know he's alone when the end comes.

I'm lining up my shot, square in the center of Blaine's dark brown bowler derby when the roar of an engine shatters the stillness of the night. Tires squeal and the buzz saw rip of a Tommy Gun assaults my ears. I see it all in perfect clarity, a sleek black sedan tears around the corner, a stream of red hot lead lancing into the Club Riviera. It's over in a heartbeat.

I track the sedan and try to get a shot off when it hits me. Three headlights, three God damn headlights! I check the scene through the scope, it's a bloody mess. Muldoon and the poor, stupid gorilla at the door are down and won't be getting up again. The .45 slugs tore them both apart. I breathe a sigh of relief when I see Danny get up, holding his left arm. He's shouting and a dozen more hoods rush out of the club, guns drawn. My chance is blown, my revenge stolen. I'm cursing a blue streak and screaming my rage at the heavens as I kick open the door to the stairwell down the building. The place is abandoned, and my angry voice echoes off the bare walls rousing the sleeping ghosts of this old building.

I'm out the back door and into the alley as the wail of sirens tears up the street. I stick to the shadows as half a dozen cop cars converge on the Club Riviera. No one is even looking my way as I stroll casually down the lane with the rifle slug over my shoulder. I'm seething inside; a ball of twisted hate is growing in my belly. I know that car; there are only fifty of them in whole damn world, a Tucker Torpedo. One man in this stinking burgh drives a Tucker Torpedo, Jimmy God Damn Knuckles!

I can't believe Vito would sanction that kind of hit. He just declared open war on the Irish Mob! The streets are going to run red with blood, and my life just got a thousand times more complicated. I'd love to kick my way into his club and ask him face to face what in God's name he was playing at, but I know that's just suicide now. I've got no choice but to head back home and try to come up with a new plan. I may not have seen any action overseas, but a new war just came home.

11. Ordinary People

My arm shudders with the impact of my gloved right hand crashing into the jaw of the palooka sharing my ring. I hit him again and he staggers back, knees wobbly, legs buckling. I step in and land a left hook and the crowd roars. The sound washes over me like a breaking wave, it's invigorating, and it reminds me what it's like to be alive. The bell rings as I move in to press the advantage, so I make my way back to my corner and plant myself on the stool "Killer" Kelly McBride shoves into the ring.

"Ah yer doin' foine dere Sonny Jim! Ya really came through for ol' Kelly dis time! Stay on him now and put him away dis round! Watch fer dat left o' his!"

Kelly is absurdly pleased with the situation. His gnarled face twists into a wide grin. He claps me on the shoulder and ducks back through the ropes. I push the mouthpiece back in and get ready to go back to work. The bell rings and I'm up and at him. It dawns on me as I land a straight right hand I've already forgotten his name. He comes at me with two hard lefts, I slip the first but the second catches me square in the eye. He's got quick hands, should have listened to Kelly. Another left comes whistling in but I duck under and land two hard shots to his midsection. He staggers again and when I hit him with a big right uppercut he goes down like a sack of bricks.

I step back to a neutral corner as the ref begins the count. Kelly is shouting and raising his knobby fists in triumph. The crowd is roaring and applauding and I'm wondering how I let myself get talked into this. It's not the first time I've subbed in on an under card, I've had my license for over a year, but it is the first time I've done it with a gang war going on outside. The ref hits ten, the crowd goes nuts and my hand gets raised in victory. There's nothing quite like it, even if the name the announcer calls out isn't my own. Kelly throws the robe on me and we make our way back to the locker room.

"Ah ya did foine dere Sonny! You took that poor palooka apart, world class son, world class! Though I can't understand why ya bother with the fake name dere son, what with that thing dere on your chest." I know he's right. The scar I carry is impossible to miss; it does a better job marking me than any name I might ever use. Back in the locker room, Kelly helps me pull off my gloves and cut the tape off my hands and wrists. I'm craving a smoke and way too tired after a four round fight.

"Pep up dere Sonny!" Kelly is still excited; sometimes I think he loves the sport of boxing more than his own kids. "Ya ought to give some thought ta doin this more regular. Ye'd be a champ for certain!"

"Kelly, I'm a little too old for that kind of career change." I'm not kidding. My fists ache and I know my right eye will be dark tomorrow.

"Yer naught but a wet behind the ears pup!"

"I'm thirty-five, Kelly!"

"Oh" He pauses for a moment to regard me thoughtfully "Now how did that go an happen? Ah, never you mind! Get yer clothes on lad, dinner's on me."

"Okay, he must have hit me harder than I thought, because I could swear you just offered to buy dinner."

"Get yer clothes on!" The old fella smiles at me, and even after taking a few shots to the face I can't help but smile back. I do as he tells me and soon enough we're in his battered old car and heading away from the arena. He can't stop talking about the fight, and I'm glad to just listen and relax for a little while. He goes over all four rounds, blow by blow, step by step. He forgets what year it is, but he can recall every punch from every fight he's ever watched. He's a strange old bird, but he's a good one.

We head into my favorite dingy diner and make for my usual booth. Kelly shakes his head at me as we take our seats.

"Swear to God boyo, do ya ever eat anyplace else?"

"Not if I can help it." I mean it. I am an orderly man, and I like what I like. When I find someplace worth going, I send them as much business as I can. I order my usual and a cup of black coffee, Kelly has the corned beef hash. He has nothing complimentary to say about it. We eat in silence for a while, broken only by Kelly's dissatisfied grunts. I'm fine with the quiet, my ears are still ringing from the punches and the cheers, so the quiet feels good. Kelly wrecks it with my least favorite words.

"I need a favor."

"Oh come on, Kelly! I just got done with one of your favors!"

"I know son, and I thank ya for that, from the bottom o' me heart. But now, now I need to ask one more thing o' ya."

"Who do you need knocked out?" I sigh. I'm not in the mood for any more violence for hire. I've got enough of it in my daily life these days.

"No, son, none o' that at all. I want ya to take over the gym when I'm gone. Since my Johnny never came back from the war and Maggie's too busy being a wife to Jack…." His voice cracks and I can see his eyes are wet, I offer him my napkin but he waves it off. "Yer the only one I trust, the only one I know will treat the her right. Ya been like one o' me own fer longer than I can recall, and now, now son dere's no one else who can do da job right." He looks at me, rheumy grey eyes watering and I know I don't have a choice.

"Okay Kelly, I'd be honored." He smiles and reaches across the table to take my hand in one of his bony paws.

"Yer a good lad, always have been! Broke me heart when Maggie decided to go with Jack."

"Kelly that was the smartest choice she ever made. It saved her life." Now it's my turn to ache.

"I know I've said it a hundred times, but I'm sorry son, I truly am. Gina was a fine woman." He gives my hand a squeeze. "No man should have ta go through what ya did." He pauses for a moment, before deciding to go on. "This thing yer doin now, it won't bring her back, son." My moment of weakness is over and my heart hardens again. Memories of fire and pain and the last night of her life burn it black.

"They have to pay Kelly, Danny Doyle and all his lackeys." My voice is cold and dispassionate, the icy scythe of winter. I'm not trying to make a scene, though there's few here to witness it. "It won't be long now, not long until I'm finished."

"Da problem is, day'll more'n likely finish you."

"They had their chance, they won't get another." Kelly lets go of my hand and we finish our meal in silence. Tonight was a nice break, a chance to feel like ordinary people again. Tomorrow, life goes on.

12. Snake

There are not many men I trust in this city; Bill Burke is one of them. He's also the only man I ever met with an uglier scar than mine. Difference is he took a hunk of shrapnel for Uncle Sam. He's got a hell of a story about it too, if you get a chance, have him tell you sometime. For now, he's sharing my booth in the back of the Deuce of Clubs and splitting a bottle of Franklin's finest with me.

"Hell of a fight Saturday." He says to me, knocking back a shot of the dark brown liquor.

"Yeah, wasn't too bad." I match his shot with one of my own. He's been here nearly an hour now, making small talk. It's his way; he gets to the point when he feels like it, no use in pushing the issue. I light a lucky and offer him the pack, he nods his thanks and lights up. Two more thin wisps of smoke join with dozens of others making the Deuce of Clubs into a hazy landscape of the desperate and the dammed. It beats being outside, a new storm rolled in and it's frozen hell in the streets.

"The Old Man wants a meeting." So now we get to it.

"The Old Man told me I wasn't much welcome anymore." It shames me to admit it, but he was right to do it. He risked starting a war with the Doyle gang by pointing me to Tommy Monaghan. As things stand, I'm wondering why he bothered.

"He understands that, and he offers you his apologies. His sincere apologies." I sit up straighter, my attention grabbed forcibly. Vito Candolini hasn't apologized to another human being in more than thirty years.

"Where and when?"

"Tomorrow, 7pm, you know the place." I nod to him, I most assuredly do. We share a few more hours of small talk and bourbon until Franklin rings the last call and throws us out into the night. The night is as cold and white as any I can remember. It's the kind of night that keeps any sane man home under a pile of blankets or in front of the fireplace. It's beautiful and terrible and painfully silent. It's a long, slow, bitterly cold walk home, but it's the most peaceful night on the streets in weeks. For that simple fact, I'm grateful for the storm. I'm frozen to the core by the time I reach my dingy little apartment.

Sleep comes easily for a change, or maybe I'm just freezing to death. Either way I'm out in a flash, sleeping like the dead. The morning comes; the light shines thin and grey though the growing layer of clouds hanging above my city. A look out the window confirms that the snow hasn't stopped. I shower and pour myself the hottest cup of coffee I can manage. I let the dark warmth fill me before I bundle up and head out into the blizzard. It is a long, frozen day and by the time evening rolls around I could not be more prepared to go someplace warm and have a decent meal.

Carmine "Moose" Mussolini, Vito's bodyguard and driver is waiting for me just inside the door of Antonelli's. Carmine is a mountain of a human being; he towers over me, looming in the dim light of the restaurant. Carmine has been the brick wall between The Old Man and the world for going on twenty years now, and it shows. He carries the scars a man in his line of work should, and it only makes him more fearsome.

"Hey there Moose, the Old Man ready for me?" I keep my tone light and friendly. I'm suspicious as hell of this whole meeting, but don't want to let on. Moose nods and leads me back into the restaurant. The place is quiet and mostly empty; Vito may well be the only diner in the building. The Old Man sees us; he waves me over and dismisses Moose in a single gesture. I offer my hand, but Vito stands and gives me a hug.

"Sit, sit, enjoy some dinner. You look like you need it!" I sit and join him in the dinner laid before us. We don't talk, not a word is exchanged until the plates are cleared and the Brandy is poured.

"Why am I here Vito?" I've got a sick feeling in my gut, and it has nothing to do with the dinner. Something is very wrong here. Vito sighs, and for the first time in my recollection he looks, old. The wrinkles that line his face look deeper, the bags under his eyes much darker, as he bends forward, head down. For all the world he looks like a beaten man.

"This God damn snake of a nephew of mine! He doesn't have enough? We got the unions, the fights, gambling, nightclubs! What the hell else does a man need? It's never enough for people like him; they don't know how to appreciate what they got! They don't know who their friends are. He thought it was time we pushed out the other gangs, says he's tired of sharing what oughtta be ours! All his book learning, all his big words and not a lick of sense in him!" Vito looks angry and sad and tired, things Vito "The Shark" Candolini should never be. I don't know what to say, so I stay quiet and let him continue. Something else catches my ear, something familiar…

"You know how this is, how our family works. You, me and Jimmy are the only three people who know I didn't order the hit on Danny Doyle. That's how it's gotta be." Vito takes a long drink of the brandy. "I wanted to say I'm sorry, for turning my back on you. Y…" He doesn't get to finish.

I launch myself at him and drag him to the floor as the room fills with a stream of white hot death. The front window shatters into a thousand shards as the room floods with the roar of a Thompson being emptied. Our booth shreds to splinters, sawdust rains down us. I'm forcing Vito's head to the floor when the torrent stops. Someone is screaming, a ragged piercing cry that stabs into my ears though the ringing buzz of the fading shots. I'm sprinting to the door as a black sedan tears down the icy road, tires struggling for purchase. It fishtails badly as it rounds the next corner and I get a good look at the front of the car. It stops me dead in my tracks. Three headlights, three God damn headlights!

The screaming has stopped and I can see why. Moose is down, and he won't be getting up again. Vito is on the floor, kneeling over his body. He looks up at me, eyes watering and we lock gazes for moment. My nod tells him all he needs to know. Jimmy Knuckles has just tried to rub him out.

13. I'll be With Her Soon

I see her looking at me, whispering behind her hand to her friends at their table. She approaches me, shyly, asking if I am who she thinks I am. I tell her I am, and invite her to join me. I'm dining alone, and could use the company. She sits across from me. We don't leave until the restaurant closes. She says her name in Gina; it's the last time I dine alone.

She smiles at me, radiant as the summer sun in her flowing white dress. Her eyes shine as she says I do, the crowd cheers and claps as we kiss. I know this is the most perfect, most beautiful day of my life. We walk arm and arm down the aisle, surrounded by our loved ones. I'm warm in my black tuxedo.

I stand in the doorway, watching her sing and hold her belly. She notices me, and grins as she sings to our little girl. She's sure we're having a daughter. I don't argue. I join her on the couch and hold her hand as she sings to our unborn child. Her voice is musical, full of a mother's love. She is everything I ever wanted. It is my last day in the sun.

I'm lying on the floor, I can't breathe. There are men in our house. I'm trying to crawl to her. It's so hard, everything hurts, the smoke is thick and black, and I can't breathe! Something is pulling me away from her. I see her face, so still, her eyes lifeless. I try to scream, to tell them to leave me, to beg them to let me stay with her but I can't breathe! They pull and pull and pull. The world goes black.

She's lying in a casket. Its dark wood is polished to a glossy sheen, catching the noon sun. The lid is closed; no one should see her like this. People I've never met clutch my hand and tell me how sorry they are, how much they feel for my loss. I'm too weak to stand. The pain in my chest has nothing to do with the bullet that nearly ended my life. They lower her down, down into the darkness she always feared. I tell her I'll be with her soon.

I'm holding the gun, it is old and heavy but it calms me. I've cleaned and oiled the revolver; it is as good as new. It has one final task. It once belonged to her father; she knew how much I love old things. She thought I'd enjoy it. I hold it to my temple, there is no fear, only relief. I shut my eyes and squeeze the trigger. The hammer rises, the cylinder turns, the hammer falls, nothing! I squeeze again and again! There is only silence, silence that brings me to my knees. I beg her to forgive me; I know what she needs me to do.

I see myself in the mirror; there is blood on my hands. I don't recognize the face staring back at me. His eyes are haunted and cold; he has done something terrible this night. The blood runs down the drain, I scrub and scrub. My hands are not clean; they can never be clean again. There is no turning back now. Outside the snow falls covering a body that was once a man. He is the first of far too many.

Tonight the snow is still falling. The gun hangs heavy and cold from its holster on my shoulder. I know I'll need it soon. I step out into the night, a night that will bring me one step closer. I tell her I'll be with her soon.

14. The Choices We Make

Somewhere out in the frozen hell that we call a city, Jimmy Knuckles is hiding. Somewhere he is cowering in the dark like the spineless worm he is. Tonight though, tonight I don't care a lick. I've restored the king to his throne, and I get to be the hero for a day.

We're in the back of his club, away from the masses and the high rollers out enjoying the show. It's just me and the Old Man, stuffing our faces and smoking the finest cigars his money could buy. He hasn't stopped talking since I showed up, I don't much mind.

"I don't know how you knew, but you knew! You smelled that rat commin'! Anything you want, anything in the world and you can have it!" He lifts his glass to me again; I smile and lift mine in return.

"I don't need anything from you Vito. You've already done enough for me."

"Everyone needs something from me! That's how I got here!" Vito laughs, but I know he's right. "Well, eat up, drink up! Enjoy yourself! Its first class for you from now on, everyday!"

"Thanks Old Man, you're only half as bad as the papers make you out to be, maybe less." He laughs and I laugh. It feels good to be his friend again. "Like you never even threw me out."

"That's something I've been meaning to talk to you about. You don't gotta do this by yourself! It won't be long before there isn't one single Mick gangster left in this city!"

"I know Vito."

"I know Vito he says!" He looks at me with a sad kind of look, like I'm his idiot son, who just never quite gets it, a combination of pity and shame and sorrow. "All this is gonna do is get yourself dead, that what good do you do then huh? None!"

"It's what she wants, Vito." The tone changes abruptly and this is a lot less like a celebration.

"Again with this? Again!" Vito pounds our table with his fist, making our plates and glasses clink and rattle. "You don't get it, you never get it! You ought to be dead! You should be a pile of rotten meat and bones in box right now but you aren't! Most men get shot by Danny Doyle, they don't get up again, but you, you! Here you are, still breathing, still fighting! Now you wanna go give him another chance, but this time he's gonna put two in your God damn brain to make sure you don't come back to bother him no more!" Vito's face is red with rage, he's not done, so I stay quiet.

"You get a second chance and you're just gonna piss it away! You're the smartest, toughest bastard I know and all you got in your head is joining your god damn wife in the dirt!" He sighs heavily and slumps back in his chair. "Get the fuck outta here; I can't stand to look at you right now."

I do as he asks, and get up ready to leave. He stops me.

"Look, you have a choice here, son. You don't gotta go get yourself killed. We'll take care of this, you, me and the rest of the boys. Doyle ain't got a chance in hell of living through this." Vito gives me that same sad look. "You gave me another chance; let me return the favor, huh?"

"I should go, got a lot to do."

"Yeah, yeah you should. God dammit." As I take my leave, I can still hear him grumbling under his breath. I pass through the club unnoticed, the patrons lost in a world of vice and joy. I don't begrudge them one minute of it. I remember how it felt. We all have choices, and we're defined by the choices we make. I've already made mine.

15. The Devil Himself

It's been three days and no one has seen hide nor hair of Jimmy Knuckles. I'm starting to think he has more sense than I ever gave him credit for. He's probably a thousand miles away and looking to get further. Two of Vito's boys found his Tucker Torpedo down by the harbor, but I'm willing to bet he ran west. I'd heard him say more than once that he'd seen enough of Europe in the War.

I've been at the Deuce of Clubs all night, hoping Bill Burke would make an appearance. His face is about as familiar as mine around here. He hasn't been in his office all week, so he's either on a case or he skipped town as well. I'm hoping it's the former. It's a slow night in the bar, the long grind of a bitterly cold winter is starting to get to even the regulars. I barely notice the time tick off my watch and before I know it Franklin is ringing the bell for last call. I finish my beer and head out into the night.

The clouds have parted just enough to let a few silver shafts of moonlight down into the city. For a minute, it's almost beautiful. I turn to head home when I hear a voice from behind that makes me freeze in my tracks.

"Now why would a gentleman such as yerself be drinkin' in a establishment like that?" I spin on my heel .38 out and ready. He's standing there, right behind me, the Devil himself.

"Shouldn't you be cowering someplace dark, Doyle?" Danny Doyle stands calmly, hands clad in fine leather gloves raised. His long coat is hanging open, his shoulder holster empty. "I'd have thought you'd have a few things on your mind."

"Me? No, I've not a care in the world! Well, not one save you, which I'm hoping to see to presently." He stands there smiling at me from beneath his bowler derby and his ludicrous red mustache. I want to gun him down in the street like the mad dog he is, it'd be so easy but it's not his time.

"What makes you think I'll give you the chance?"

"Oh please boyo, I know your kind to well! You fancy yerself on a righteous mission of vengeance; yer not the kind of animal to shoot an unarmed man down in the street. Now here it is, I know I wronged you. I took that pretty wife and that child in her belly from you fair enough. I'm here to make amends!" He says those last words and his grin just gets wider. It takes everything I have not to finish him off right here and now.

"Make amends! You sick son of a bitch!" I step in and drill him right in his grinning face with a hard left hand, he spins and drops. The gun shakes in my hand. "You took everything from me you bastard, everything!" He spits blood into the snow, the crimson freezing to pink.

"Everything? No boyo not by half!" He's laughing now, laughing! "What about that crazy old McBride? Or maybe his pretty little daughter and her husband the fighter? How about that darkie in the bar there you seem so bloody fond of? How about the green eyed bitch that stole me money? She'll pay for that, believe me!" He's up now, bloody grin flashing the moonlight. "You've lots more to lose and I'll take every one o' them from ya before I'm done!" He raises his arms in a motion of mad triumph. "Though ya can save every one o' them right now, just walk away! I don't care where ya go or what ya do just you fuck right off, right now! Get out of *my* city and never come back!"

"Even if I go, Vito will carve you up and feed you to fish. You'll never be safe Doyle, not for one minute of your god forsaken life." My words come out cold, harsher than the frozen winter night but the grinning fiend just laughs.

"I've already won ya daft fuck! You'll get no aid from Vito Candolini! There's no one left but you!" he laughs again, the sickening sound of a Loon gone mad. "But since I'm a gentleman of my word I'll give you one last chance to leave of your own accord!"

"You're insane, Doyle! I just saved the Old Man's life."

"You ought to read more boyo, be good for your world image!" He reaches slowly into his coat and tosses me the paper that was tucked into his belt. I keep him covered while I unfold it with my free hand. My eyes go wide at the headline.

Local Gangster to Turn State's Evidence, the end of the Candolini Mob!

Danny Doyle sees the shock on my face and turns to go. I call out to him and he turns to face me, still wearing the bloody Cheshire grin.

"Ready to see reason are y…" The rapport of my .38 cuts him off, his words turning into a scream of rage and agony. He slumps into the snow, clutching a spouting left knee. I kneel next to him, smoke still coming from the barrel of my pistol.

"You don't know me at all Danny. I didn't kill you because I want you to suffer. I didn't kill you because I want you to know what hell is Danny Doyle." I hear footsteps, running towards us, and I know it's time to go. I rush off into the night, I'll see him again. We aren't nearly done.

16. No One Ever Listens

Have you ever run through day old snow in a pair of wingtips? I don't recommend it. On occasion, you don't have much of a choice. A bullet cracks past by my head, I duck instinctively. It's another near miss. The good news is, they're slipping as much as I am, bad news is there are five of them. Two more bullets tear past my head as I duck down the next alley I see. I need to find someplace to take cover and make a stand. I'm done running.

It's dark as pitch in the alley and full of debris from the crumbling building to my left. This whole neighborhood was scheduled for demolition before the winter came in all her terrible glory. The lights on this block haven't worked in months. The bright full moon is reduced to a pale, dim glow by the thick layer of clouds above. In short, it's perfect. I crouch low behind a pile of tumbled bricks and wait for my chance. It's not long in coming.

Doyle's men aren't stupid, they're killers all and most of them saw action in the war. I can barely make them out in the darkness, dark suits blending with the darker night. No one wants to be the first into the breach, they spread out and take what cover they can near the mouth of alley. I hold my fire; as soon as I pull the trigger my night vision is gone. At least it's not snowing. I feel the first frozen flake on the back of my neck a moment later. Of course, why not? This is not my day.

"Hey!" One of the thugs shouts "Hey! Can we move this along already? It's snowing!" His voice echoes off the walls, coming from every which way.

"So I've noticed! Why don't you come on in so I can finish you off and go find someplace warm to be?" One of the gangsters fires into the blackness, the bullet punching into the brick wall several feet to my left. "Nope, that's not going to do it."

"Hold yer fire ya daft idiot!" The first voice shouts again.

"Look, boys, why don't you just go on home. I'd really rather not have to kill all of you. There's only seven more of you that need killin and none of you are on the list!" One more shot rings out, this one high and to the right.

"Goddammit hold yer fire! Look lad, tis either we bring Danny yer head, or he'll have ours. Simple as that."

"What's your name?" He pauses for a moment; I can almost see the look on confusion on his face.

"Mallory, Peter Mallory."

"How long you been in the States Peter?" He's totally lost now, I can feel it. Dark silhouettes turn to glance at one another as I shift silently towards the tumbled down building on my left hand side. Sliding silently into a gaping doorway, the wooden door long left to rot, forgotten. The interior is mostly clear, I move silently through it, making my way carefully to the front door.

"Since the war's end. Once I was out o' the army going back to the farm seemed like a dismal way to spend my remainin' years."

"Peter, what the hell are you doing?" One of the gangsters asks him a loud hissing whisper. They don't think I can hear them, they don't realize I'm already next to them.

My .38 barks and one of the men drops like a ton of bricks. A second shot takes down another as they turn, the bullet hitting him square in the forehead. By the time they react I'm already in amongst them! A close range fire fight is a horrific thing, it's all muzzle flashes, heat and horror. I dodge and turn, lashing out it all directions, never letting them gets a clean shot off. I feel the burn of a graze, a streak of fire shooting across my right shoulder. I fire again; I can hear a gun clatter to the floor and howl of agony. Shots roar into the night, the sound pounds my brain like a sledgehammer; it crushes into my ears until there is only silence. I feel, rather than hear my revolver click as the hammer strikes a spent cartridge.

There's only one of them left standing, I see white teeth in the darkness as he grins and raises his weapon. Click! I'm on him before he can move my switchblade in hand. I drive it home between his ribs, plunging the blade in deep! He lets out a gasp as he collapses. I lower him gently to the ground as his struggles gradually subside. The night is even darker now; the multiple muzzle flashes have ruined my night eyes. I nearly trip on Peter Mallory, he sits clutching his right hand to his chest. His dark shirt stained darker with blood. I sit down next to him in the gathering snow.

"You ok?" I'm shouting despite myself, the silence has become a loud roar as my ears come back to life.

"What?" he shouts back, a distant whisper behind the tumult. I shake my head and pull my pack of Luckys from my coat pocket. I offer him one and he nods his head in agreement. I light us up and we wait in silence, two ghouls amongst the dead, covered in blood, until we can communicate once again.

"Let me see your hand." I say, when the ringing has faded somewhat. He holds out his right hand, it's a bloody mess. "Well, looks like you won't be giving anyone the bird anytime soon." He won't, one of the shots has torn his middle finger clean off.

"Ah, hurts less than I thought it might! Why'd ya have to go and shoot off me finger?"

"Well, I can still put one in your brain if you like. Besides, you ruined a perfectly good coat."

"Ya have a way of makin' a man see reason." I search the bodies of the fallen, pulling wallets free as blood begins to freeze in the chill of the night air. I clean out all the cash and toss the roll of bills to Mallory.

"Peter, get out of my city. Take that and go, I don't care

where. This city is Hell; it will destroy you like it has everything else it touches. Good men come here to die, and evil men to pick their bones." He nods, I hope he understands. I stand and place another smoke in his remaining good hand. "I want you to look around yourself. I want you to remember what you see." I wait as he does, the clouds parting just enough to let the horror of the scene play out in black and white before us. Four dead men, four wasted lives, four futures obliterated in moments. I can see his eyes go wide for a moment before the clouds thicken and wash all detail from the scene. "You never saw combat did you, Peter?"

"No" his voice is small now, quiet. "I spent the war behind a desk. I was a translator." I nod, I don't know if he can see me.

"Neither did I. I was home fat and happy, hawking war bonds and playing the cheerleader. The War Department felt it'd be bad for the nation's morale if I went and got myself killed. I never fired a weapon in anger until I came back to this hellhole." I give him a light as he holds the Lucky in his trembling left hand. "Last thing, I lay eyes on you again, you're dead. I don't give a man a second chance to kill me."

I don't turn to look as I walk away. He won't shoot me in the back; I can already tell he's not the type. I hope he'll get it. I hope he'll go home and live a life of peace and quiet. Something tells me I'll see him again. No one ever listens.

17. The Abyss

My hands ache. I look down at my split and blood covered knuckles and for a moment I forget they belong to me. I don't remember them looking like this, ragged, torn and scarred. My sleeves are rolled up past my elbows, but there is still blood everywhere. It's up my arms, all over my tie, sprayed across my once clean white shirt. The sight of it would shock a sane mind, it barely registers in mine.

The ache that started in my hands spreads all through me, creeping like morphine through my veins. I'm not sure how long I've been at this now, it feels like days. Every bit of me is sore and bone weary. The cold I had stopped noticing is seeping back into my pores. It draws a shiver as my sweat starts to freeze. Where's my coat?

I find it crumpled on the dirty floor of the supposedly abandoned warehouse that had been the scene for tonight's horrors. I heard that Sean Flynn had been using it to store some of the Doyle Gang's less than legal acquisitions. I had never expected to find this kind of stash, disguised behind broken windows and chipping paint.

The government shut down Fort Stendelman not long after V - J Day. Without a word or an explanation to anyone in town they had moved out every item of value and bulldozed the place flat. All that was left was the fence full of signs warning everyone to stay the hell off or get shot. They've been building every summer since, God only knows what. Most people don't ask. We figure it's none of our damn business, that's just how it is here. Keep your head down and don't ask any questions. Well, it would appear not everything from the base made it out of town. This warehouse is presently home to crates upon crates of things no honest criminal should ever need. Grenades, cases of Comp B, several light machine guns, dozens of Thompsons and thousands upon thousands of rounds, its insanity! I have no idea what Doyle was going to use any of this for but it's terrifying to think he had it this whole time and no one noticed. Small wonder the guards here hadn't fired a shot.

I don't mind not being shot at, fact of the matter is it makes my life much easier, but when you ambush a pair of gorillas in cheap suits guarding an "abandoned" warehouse you expect them to squeeze off a few rounds. I let them run for their lives; they aren't why I came here. They aren't on the list. My eyes got wide when I saw what they were guarding; it suddenly made a lot more sense as to why they were so unusually terrified of man with a gun.

It wasn't hard to find Flynn; I could hear him muttering to himself as soon as I slid in the door. I kept quiet and got an eye full of the joint before I approached him. He was checking crates one by one; making sure not a single thing had been misplaced. Sean had always been a numbers man, a detail guy. I could hear him grumbling about the cold as I made my way behind him. The click of my .38's hammer made him stand bolt upright. He turned slowly, until he was staring down the barrel of my pistol.

"Fer God's sake ya madman, put that thing away! You'll blow us all ta kingdom come!" I didn't speak, I didn't have to. He knew why I was there. I hit him with a hard left hand and he collapsed to the floor. He groaned and held his jaw. "I didn't even want ta be there that night! Please! I'm no killer!" I kicked him hard in the ribs and felt a satisfying give. He curled into a ball. "I didn't even have a gun!" he gasped weakly.

I remember taking my coat off, and watching it slowly drop to the dust covered floor. I remember rolling up my sleeves before I started hitting him over and over and over. The rest is red blur of pain and blood and begging.

The wet rasp of his breathing brings me back into the present. Flynn is still alive, but only barely so. His face is shattered red mess barely recognizable as human. I don't know when he lost consciousness but it couldn't have been soon enough for him. I know

I could get him to hospital; I could spare his life, horrid though it may now be. I could step away from my slow decent to hell if only for a moment. I don't.

I can't remember where I read it, but I remember the quote all to well. "Battle not with monsters lest ye become one, and if you gaze into the abyss the abyss gazes into you." I never got philosophy, but this one I understand. There comes a point where you stop being the hero of your own story, when you realize that white hat you wear has been stained black by blood and gun smoke. I should call the cops, but by the time they bothered to show up in this neighborhood Doyle's boys would have everything moved and he'd still have enough guns to start World War III.

I get as far back as I can before I hurl the grenade. I have a pretty good arm, but the pineapple is a whole lot heavier than a baseball. I hit the dirt behind the best cover I can find, Sean's black Ford sedan and cover my ears. The roar is the voice of an angry God, the force of the building going up shatters the Ford's windows and rocks it back, threatening to tip it over onto me. Thankfully it drops back down onto four wheels and I'm only moderately sliced up by the glass shower.

The warehouse is a smoking crater full of loose bricks and flaming shards of wood, the neighboring buildings aren't much better. It's a far grander pyre than a coward like Flynn deserved. The snow will keep the fire from spreading, and none of the neighboring buildings were occupied. Danny Doyle is crazy, but not stupid. He would never hide an arsenal like that anywhere that someone might have stumbled on it. I hope to God it's the only one he's got. I take a moment to commit the scene to memory. I want to remember the day I first noticed the abyss staring back.

18. Do Something Right

It's two days after Christmas and 1949 is about to be a memory. I can't say I'm going to miss this decade. The wind is howling outside, but thankfully it hasn't brought more snow. There's already a foot or more of it covering everything that happened to stand still in the last twenty-four hours. I watch it all through the very foggy glass of a diner I had never been inside before today. The wind rattles the glass, and I slide casually to the far end of my booth. I've finally stopped feeling the burn of the thousand little cuts from my last run in with shattering glass, and I am not eager to go through days of Iodine and stitches again.

This new place is a little better lit than I prefer, but the menu looks promising. I'm a creature of habit, always have been. When I find a joint I like I tend to become a regular. Right now, that's just short of suicidal. I haven't been to the Deuce of Clubs in weeks and I'm actually starting to miss Franklin's cheap beer and cheaper whiskey. I stare out the window at the empty street and feel very much like I'm the only person awake in the whole damn city. A voice from behind reminds me that I'm not.

"Do you know what you'd like?" The waitress is tall and very blond. Even without her accent I can tell she's not from around here. They don't grow them like her in a city of perpetual gray.

"Iowa?" I ask, eyebrow raised. She squints, peering at me quizzically through shockingly blue eyes.

"Kansas." She answers. I nod.

"How's the ham steak?"

"Terrible."

"Okay" I scan the menu "How about the eggs?"

"Very runny."

"The chicken fried steak?"

"The worst I've ever had."

"Well, either you're very new at the whole waitress game or I've stumbled into the worst diner in the city." She glances around the room, I follow her gaze. It dawns on me that the place is completely empty. I'm not real sure how I missed that. "Well…..what do you recommend? It's about minus ten outside and I really don't feel like going to look for another all night diner."

"Junior is passed out drunk back there, but I can tell you the Chili is hot and passably fresh."

"Well, with a recommendation like that, how could I refuse?" She smiles and makes for the counter. I turn my attention back to the ominously rattling window. She's returned before I know it with a bowl of steaming hot chili con carne. I had gotten a taste for the stuff as I toured through the southwest and California. This…is a sorry impostor.

"How is it?"

"Exactly as advertised."

"I'm sorry. Can I get you anything else?"

"Coffee, black and strong as you got."

"Sure thing."

"Actually, grab one for yourself and come take a break. I'm sure you could use one after this rush of business." She smiles at me again and brings back two steaming mugs of hot coffee. The strong black liquid washes some of the horrid taste out of my mouth. She slides into the booth across from me.

"You were right, after all that work, I'm bushed!" she giggles at her own joke. It's surprisingly endearing.

"So, let's have it. How does a Kansas girl like yourself end up in the worst diner, in the worst city on the eastern seaboard, working the midnight shift with a drunk 'Junior' passed out in the kitchen?" Her smile fades a little.

"It's a long story mister; you wouldn't want to hear it." I wave my head towards the window. She turns to look as the first snowflakes begin to impact against the window, propelled by the fierce wind.

"I'm not going back out in that anytime soon, and I sincerely doubt you're going to be to terribly busy the rest of the night. I don't mean to pry, but I figure we've got some time to kill." She sighs and nods her head

"It's a not a very original story. A girl meets a boy from the wrong side of the tracks. She doesn't care very much about any of that, because she very much in love." She stares off over my shoulder, getting lost in the memory. "Her parents disapprove, but she's young and confident that love can solve anything. Things move on, and he falls in with a bad crowd. She follows him, she's sure it won't last. She tells herself that he's not really a bad man, he's just a little lost."

Her eyes lose some of the faraway dream-like quality they've had. I sit quietly and sip my coffee as she continues.

"Things get worse, as they tend to do. He gets deeper and deeper into a world he doesn't belong to. He sees things, does things…" her voice drifts and I see her eyes water for moment, but she continues on. "He comes home one night, drunk and angry. She tries to calm him down, tries to help the boy she loves so much. She gets a black eye for her trouble. In the morning, when he's sober and calm he tells her how sorry he is, how he never meant to hit her. He begs for forgiveness, and she give it. She knows he didn't mean it. A few weeks later he comes home with blood on his shirt, she asks if he's okay, if he's been hurt. She gets a bloody mouth for her trouble."

My knuckles turn white as I grip the coffee cup. I'm thankful this dump had solid mugs or I might be bloody and wearing my coffee.

"It's the same the next morning. It's all the same, and she forgives him. This time he doesn't even wait a week. He comes home in the middle of the night, his eye is swollen and black, his jacket is torn and bloody. She tries to help him, to take care of him, but he pulls out a gun she never even knew he had and calls her terrible names. He tells her to mind her own business or he will teach her to mind it. This time, she waits for him to pass out drunk, she takes every dollar in their little place and she goes to bus station with nothing but the clothes on her back. She buys a ticket on the next bus and rides on and on until she winds up here." She looks down for a second, at her untouched cup of rapidly cooling coffee. "I'm sorry, I don't know why I told you all that. You must not think much of me at all."

"No need to be sorry. I asked."

"You sound so familiar, are you sure you haven't been in here before?"

"Not once, but I do get that a lot." For a second, I contemplate telling her who I am, but the thought doesn't linger.

"Okay Mister, what's your story? How did you end up in the worst diner in town in the middle of the worst night of 1949?" It comes at me again, the urge to tell her everything, the whole story. I don't know what the hell is wrong with me.

"I don't think you'd believe me if I told you." I chuckle a little, trying to hide my discomfort.

"Oh no! You are not getting off that easy! I may not be from the big city but I wasn't born yesterday!" She notices my empty mug, and how cold hers has gotten. "I am going to get us some fresh coffee, and you are going to spill it Mister!" She takes my cup and heads back to the kitchen. I stare out the window while I wait for her to return. I watch the frozen crystals crash and cling to the window, a layer of ice building and growing, crawling over the glass like a living thing, consuming every inch of it. It's not hard to make my decision. She comes back with our coffee and eases her way into the booth across from me. She smiles at me as I meet those too blue eyes.

I tell her everything. From the night Gina was murdered, to the incident at the warehouse a week ago, every bloody detail. I watch her smile fade and her brow furrow as she soaks in every word. She never interrupts me, never asks a question, she just sits and looks more and more concerned.

"So that's it, that's how I ended up in here. If you find yourself with a sudden urge to make yourself busy elsewhere I'd understand entirely."

"No" she says, reaching across the table to take my scarred and battered hand. "I asked." She pauses, her voice becoming very low; as if she's afraid someone might hear us in the empty diner. "Did you really kill all those men?" I nod. For a few more moments she doesn't say anything else, she just holds my hand and peers at me with those piercing eyes. "You must have really loved her."

"Still do."

"I hope you find some peace someday."

"I'm not sure I'd know what to do with it." She nods at me again. Our cups are empty and she goes to bring us another refill. While she's gone I take out the notebook I carried with me all through my former life. I have never seen one quite like it since I first bought it home from Italy. By the time she gets back I'm nearly done. I tear a sheet out and hand it to her as she offers me a fresh mug of Joe.

"What's this?" She looks down at my terrible scrawl.

"There's a man named Barry who works at Capitol records out in Los Angeles. He owes me a favor. That's your letter of introduction. He'll get you a job and help you find someplace to live."

"What? Los Angeles?" She looks up me, completely confused.

"He'll know the writing, and he'll know the paper." I take out my wallet and unfold three hundred dollar bills. "This looks like a fair tip." I take my hat and coat from the seat next to me and slide out of the booth. She catches my hand as I'm pulling on my coat.

"I can't….I mean….why would you do this?" Those too blue eyes plead with me to sit, to stay here with her.

"You don't belong here." I gently pull my hand away and finish putting on my coat and hat. I step out into the snow and immediately feel the cold wind bite. She stands in the doorway as I melt into the storming night. I know she'll go, and I pray she'll have the kind of life she deserves. For the first time in weeks I actually feel good about myself. Just goes to show you, sometimes even a wreck like me can do something right.

19. To Kill a Killer

The streets of the city are quiet tonight. A shroud hangs over her, dark and silent as the grave. The little people hide themselves away to wait the morning, as gray and cold as it may come. It has to be better than the night. A madman stalks the streets. An injured animal is the most dangerous kind, but when I first saw Doyle with his new cane I couldn't help but smile. He's angrier than ever, and the streets are full of his killers.

Danny Doyle inspires fear, because he doesn't care what he does, or to whom he does it. People see him laughing while he stabs a man to death and they know it could just as easily be them. Patty O'Shaughnessy is a different kind of monster.

It's said some men have ice water in their veins, Patty skips the water. Word on the street is no one has ever seen him show one hint of emotion. He's killed over a dozen people and the expression on his face has never changed. He's the closest thing to a real life automaton I've ever seen, and now I'm crouched across the street and looking for a way into his hideout.

I've been here for nearly an hour now; if not for the four black sedans parked out front, the building I'm watching would appear completely abandoned. There's no shortage of derelict buildings in this city. The war brought prosperity everywhere across America, except here it seems. They haven't been in long; the engines of the cars are still steaming in the frozen air. There are at least sixteen men in the building, probably more but I've got no way to be sure. They put blackout curtains in every window during the war, and these have never come down. Patty's boys are sharp, he doesn't tolerate anything less.

I'm about to make my way around to the back of building when movement by the door stops me in my tracks. A half-dozen grumbling, dark suited men pile out the front door and into the waiting sedans. A cloud of frozen breath and cigarette smoke lingers by the door as it swings casually shut. I can make out their faces as they pile into two of the cars, Patty must still be inside. Can I really be this lucky?

The pair of dark sedans pulls away and into the night. I wait until the last hint of their headlights vanish before I make my move. I jog across the street, my shoes crunching the snow and ice beneath my soles. I'm across the street quickly and up against the darkened warehouse. I can hear muffled voices from the other side of the door, there are at least two men just inside. I'm about to make my way to the back when the door swings open wide! Into the frozen night steps Patty O'Shaughnessy.

We both pause for a second, he looks at me, I look at him and neither of us moves for a few agonizing heartbeats. We go for our guns and my .38 is out before he can get his gloved hand into his heavy coat. He stares unblinking, expression unchanged, down the barrel of my revolver.

"So, it's my time is it?" he asks. I cock the hammer. "Before you do that, I believe I have something you might want to hear."

"Let me guess, all those boys you just sent off will be returning immediately and I'll never get away with this?" I grin at my own clever wit.

"No, they're off ta see your old friend McBride. They'll not be back soon. If ya leave now, ya may yet get there in time to do something about it. If ya shoot me, you'll have ta fight with every man left inside there an if ya' want ta mix it up wit' me, ya'll never make it." He's right and if he's sent his killers after Kelly then I don't have a second to spare. I step in and clock him in the face with the handle of my pistol! He drops like a sack of bricks, blood pouring from his nose, keys clinking from his gloved hand into the snow.

I snatch them up off the blood covered snow and run to the

first of the two sedans, my shoes sliding on the slick, icy concrete. I jam the key into the door and thankfully it clicks. The car rumbles briefly before it turns over. I see Patty in the rear view mirror, groggily getting to his feet. The tires spin on the ice before they catch and I fishtail off into the night. I drive like a mad man, swerving and barely under control on the icy slick streets. I ignore every red light, every traffic sign; I turn the wrong way down one way streets. I need to be there first!

McBride's Gym comes into view; I see the two sedans, engines still steaming. There's a dark figure by the door, trying to stay in the shadows. I aim the car right at him and punch the gas. He looks up and his eye get big as saucers, I dive out the driver's side door as all two thousand pounds of American steel plow into him. The solid double doors explode inward as the car tears into the gym. I roll as best I can on the slick surface, but I feel something slip in my shoulder as I crash into the front of the gym. I scramble to my feet as shouts of alarm come from inside the darkened gym.

I'm on my feet and around to the back of the building before anyone makes it past the upended car and out front. My right shoulder throbs, I can move my arm but it burns like holy hell. I take my .38 in my left hand, pulling it awkwardly from my shoulder holster. There only one man left out back. He's sticking his head in the back door and paying absolutely no attention to me. I bring the handle of my pistol down as hard as I can manage on the back of his head. He pitches forward into the darkness, collapsing with a soft thump. I make out five dark forms in the dim streetlight that now pours in through the gaping hole that was McBride's front door.

"Mary, Mother a' Jesus what a mess!" I can hear one say "What the hell happened?"

"Looks like some wanker lost control a' his car." another answers.

"If he lost control, where the fuck is he?" I know I don't have long now before they look out front and find my trail. The lights are off all over the gym, but I can see a faint red glow coming from near Kelly's small office. As silently as I can I creep across the gym, I holster my gun and dig my knife out of my coat pocket, the effort causing fire to shoot up my injured arm. Crouching low, I make my way closer to the red glow, until I can clearly make out the silhouette of someone smoking.

He's looking away from me, at the ruin of the front door. I slide up nice and quiet. I clamp my left hand over his mouth and jam the stiletto in between his ribs. He struggles but his knees swiftly go weak He nearly drags me to the floor as he collapses, my right arm can barely hang on to the knife as I lower him down. The office is dark and quiet, the door hanging half open. I listen for a few heartbeats, but hear nothing but my own slow breathing. I make my way inside, but I can't see a damn thing in the pitch blackness. Thankfully my Zippo is my left coat pocket; I ease the door shut as I flick it to life.

The room comes alive with subtle, dancing shadows. The shade is pulled on the single window on the office door. I'm hoping it will keep my presence here a secret for a few more moments. I scan the room and almost miss him. He's huddled in the corner, and he's not moving! I shut the lighter and crouch down next to Kelly. I put my hand down in a puddle of blood and I already know I'm too late. Kelly's not breathing, and he lost so much blood..... He's dead, and it's all my fault. I pull my pistol and make my way back to the door. I ease the door open, just in time to see dark shapes entering from the back door. The one in the lead shouts as he tumbles forward. Well, now they know for sure I'm in here with them.

"Johnny? What the hell?" the one of the floor shouts. Now's my chance! I rush across the gym while their eyes adjust to the darkness! By the time they hear me I'm on top of them! My shoe comes crashing down on the face on the one lying on the floor, he shrieks as I feel the cartilage in his nose snap! I bring my gun up and fire three times, the thunder of the gun is deafening in the small gym. The blindingly bright muzzle flashes have turned me into a bat. After a few second my vision clears, and since I'm still standing I'm assuming they aren't.

The one whose nose I stomped into his skull is still rolling on the floor groaning. I grab him by the collar and drag him to his feet, I'm angry beyond reason and don't even notice my right arm's protestations. I haul him into the office and fling him bodily down next to Kelly.

"You fucking bastard! You killed a harmless old man, you fuck!" I kick him hard in the ribs and he coughs wetly. He tries to talk but he just spits out another wet cough. I holster my pistol and flip open my knife. I yank his hair back hard, slamming the back of his head into the back wall of Kelly's office. I drag the knife slowly across his throat and I watch as the life drips from him. I put one it he back of the head of the unconscious thug at the back door, before tumbling out the door. Someone must have called the cops by now; God knows they'd pick now to show.

I stagger out into the snow, the savage cold reminding me of my injured shoulder. I'm not even a hundred yards away before my knees buckle and I heave my guts out. Kelly is dead! The tears come hot and angry. I sob like a child for the first time since my wife's funeral. Those bastards killed the kindest old man I'd ever known. They killed him, and it's all my fault.

20. Nothing but Trouble

I didn't go to Kelly's funeral. I know Danny Doyle had men watching the whole goings on, and they wouldn't hesitate to gun down every man, woman and child there if it meant killing me as well. So here I am to pay my respects.

I kneel by the small headstone, brushing the freshly fallen snow away. He deserves so much more than this. At least he's with his Molly now, after all these years. I know how much he missed her. I haven't had the heart to go see Maggie and Jack. I don't even know what to say to them. "Sorry" just seems woefully inadequate. How do you apologize to someone for getting their father murdered? How do ask for forgiveness for taking away someone who means so much? I may figure it out someday, if I live to be a thousand.

I don't even know what to do now. I'd pray if I still thought I had the right. Right now, I think I'm shit out of luck with Heaven. You were a good man Kelly McBride, I'm only sorry you wasted so much of your life on me. You taught me how to fight; you showed me how to be a man. You kept me honest and knocked sense into me when I needed it. I miss you, you old bastard.

I catch a whiff of something on the chill breeze; it's faint but terribly familiar. The scent of Jasmine and Honeysuckle…

"What are you doing here, Delilah?" I don't even need to look to know she's made her way quietly behind me.

"Oh you are simply no fun at all! Aren't you even a teensy bit surprised to see me?"

"I would be if you ever changed your perfume. Aren't you supposed to be in Paris?" I turn now, standing and stretching. There stands Delilah the siren in all her glory, wrapped head to toe in furs that must have cost a king's ransom. Her hair is different, longer, but still raven black.

"Oh Paris was so terribly dull! I couldn't stand it a moment longer!" She affects her most absurdly bored face.

"Got into some trouble then? Who'd you rob, or did you kill someone this time?"

"That is none of your business at all!" She moves next to me, looking down on the graves. Her presence is overpowering. It has been since the first night she tried to have me killed. "So Danny killed the old buzzard? I would have thought you'd have settled this all by now! I am disappointed in you." I turn to leave.

"Will you please get out of here? Doyle is going to skin you alive for making off with his money." She matches stride for stride as we make our way out of the cemetery.

"Oh please! That incompetent bumbler? If he had anyone good enough to kill me, he wouldn't have needed to hire me to kill you!"

"Twice." I add, under my breath.

"Well! You're acting like I actually tried to kill you!"

"You nearly got me killed at the Arena!" I turn to face her, stopping dead in my tracks. "If it wasn't for Jack you'd have damn well succeeded!"

"I told you last time that was before I knew you! That doesn't count at all. Besides, all I did was get you into the dressing room. " She lowers her entirely unnecessary sunglasses and wink one of her emerald green eyes at me. All I can do is stare at her in disbelief. Honestly, I shouldn't be shocked.

"Will you please just get out of town? For God's sake you crazy woman, you're going to end up dead!"

"Awww, you do care after all!" I sigh, and exasperated,

defeated sound escaping my lips. "You're playing the big brave hero again, keeping your little damsel in distress safe from the big, bad gangster." She actually giggles and I think I'm about to lose it.

"You're not my damsel, and yes, I'd prefer if you didn't get yourself killed, as you have managed not to sell me out *almost* half the time."

"The first time simply doesn't count!"

"Why do you do this to me? Don't you have anyone else to torture?"

"You love it! You know you need me around, who else is going to help you with your Irish Mafia problem?"

"I don't need help." She turns and looks behind us, back to the graves we've just left.

"You don't?"

"That was below the belt." My voice is low and angry. "I'm sick of your games, Delilah. I'm telling you for the last time to go." For the first time since she's arrived she looks serious.

"You're right. I'm sorry; I know you cared about him. Doesn't this just scream to you that you need help? It was one thing when you had the Candolini Mob watching your back, but now it's just you. You can't fight the world alone!"

"Watch me!" I've had enough of Delilah for today. She has to be the most infuriating woman in the world. I turn towards the street without a further word. Delilah follows me in silence as we approach the wrought iron gates of the cemetery. They are massive, rust flecked things that swing creakily on hinges that have seen better days. They are terribly imposing, yet hauntingly beautiful. The bare willows that line the walls add a disturbing touch, like the bones of the dead clawing for the sky. Though, in the all too brief summer it has a very different effect. The street is nearly empty, there's nothing down this road but the old boneyard.

"Is that your car?" Delilah obliterates the blessed silence.

"I didn't…" I dive and drag her down into the snow as all hell breaks loose around us! Somewhere near by a Thompson chatters, forty-five calibers slugs chew through the cinderblock wall and rip into the dormant trees. Wood splinters and masonry disintegrates under the incoming storm, I gather Delilah as far under me as I can, keeping my face down low in the snow. The sound of lead on metal pounds my ears until I want to scream, thankfully it's soon replaced by squealing tires and deafening silence. I look down at Delilah; it seems I broke her sunglasses.

"Well, it's not quite how I imagined getting you on top of me, but I'll take it!" I can't help but roll my eyes as I help her up. She plucks up her broken sunglasses and gives me a ridiculously sad face. "Where they here for you, or me?" I point across the street to the only remaining car. They must have emptied a full drum of ammo into it, the engine is leaking fluid from a half dozen locations. It resembles Swiss cheese more than Ford in its present state.

"You, that was definitely about you." I point to shredded trees and damaged cemetery wall. "This counts as three."

"It most certainly does not!" The argument continues as we begin the long walk back to town. I'm almost happy to see Delilah, even if she is nothing but trouble.

21. Hollywood is full of Liars

I know we've all seen it in the movies, the hero of the story has his climactic battle with the black hat atop a tall building under the light of a full moon. It's beautiful, terrifically cinematic and the hero always wins. I wish the world were so black and white. That's the last thing that crosses my mind as I make way towards The Madison Building, one of the city's finest new high rise apartment buildings.

I had it on good evidence that Scotty "The Bull" Hanlon has a mistress set up with a fine little place and pays her a visit every Thursday night, without fail. It wasn't hard to convince the doorman that I had business inside as my dear old friend President Grant made the introductions for me. Soon, he, I and the doorman were all fast friends and I head up stairs.

Either Bull has really moved up in the world, or he really likes this new girl. I haven't been in a joint this nice in quite a while. The carpets are pristine and a rich purple, the brazen knob on every door gleams under soft electric lights. The stairs are solid, without a hint of squeak as I begin the long trek to the 14th floor. I avoid the elevator entirely. I've already had to bribe one person; I'd prefer to avoid making it two. The less mouths that have to keep quiet the more likely it'll happen.

I'm a little winded by the time I reach the final landing; I've been lazy since my shoulder got dislocated. I can't afford to do that anymore. I move silently down the hall, the plush purple carpeting killing the sound of my footsteps. If I'm right, they should be in number 1430. I don't hear anything as I sneak down the hall. Maybe I caught a break and everyone is asleep or out for the night. I pull my .38 as I near the door, ready for anything. I press my ear to the door, there's definitely activity inside.

I'm about to work the lock when everything goes SNAFU. Behind me someone starts shouting; I guess the floor isn't quite asleep. I turn to find a finely dressed young couple standing just outside apartment 1420. I don't look much like I belong here to begin with, the gun doesn't help. She's screaming for the police, he's standing there slack jawed and I figure I have nothing left to lose now.

I load up and kick the front door with everything I got! With a crash the cream colored door busts inward, the door frame cracking and splintering. I'm in and through, .38 at the ready. I stop short two steps into the room. Bull Hanlon has his girl by the neck with a .45 to her head and she's got nothing on but a sheet. Thank God Bull managed to get some clothes on.

"Don'tcha come no closer! I'll plug her!" Scotty is local boy, and only partly of the blood. It's a big part of why he's never moved up in the gang.

"Bull, why the hell would I care if you shot your own girl?"

"Oh…" That's the other reason. Scott is about as smart as a bag of hammers. "You ain't supposed to let nobody get killed! Four Fingers told me! You don't wanna hurt nobody you don't haveta!"

"Four Fingers?" Oh God dammit. He better not mean…

"Four Fingers Mallory, yeah! He told alla us that you ain't lookin' to kill nobody you ain't gotta! Now you just get outta here or I'm gonna plug her!"

"Bull, I'm not the one who'd be killing her, you would. That's on your head, not mine."

"Oh….." Bull shoves her forward hard. It's about the last thing I expected and I struggle to catch her, both of us tumbling to the floor. By the time I untangled from her and the sheet Bull is already out the window and onto the fire escape! Damn him, if he gets to the street he's gone for sure! I'm up and after him, quick as lighting but he surprises me again. Instead of going down, he's going up. I've got my .38 out, and I follow him cautiously. The fire escape is slick with snow and ice and it's a terribly long drop to street below. I see him clambering onto the roof, disappearing over the ledge. Right now I have two choices, go up for a sure ambush, or turn tail run. No choice at all really.

I shoulder roll over the ledge and come up in a low crouch gun at the ready. For the third time tonight Bull has caught me totally off guard! He's just standing on the roof grinning like an idiot, hands in the air!

"What the hell are you playing at Hanlon?" Then I hear it, faint on the wind, the screech of sirens.

"Da cops is on their way. I'm just a poor law abiding citizen getting held up by a crazy man. Dey all saw yous downstairs." I make my way across the roof and put the barrel of my gun right in his face.

"I don't have time for this, Bull! You tell me where O'Shaughnessy is and this is the last time you see me! If not" I cock the hammer "then I'm putting one in your brain and calling it a night."

"I don't know nuthin about nobody!"

"God damn it Bull! What the hell did he ever do for you? They treated you like the idiot little brother your whole damn life because you're a half breed. You're not one of them, you don't talk like one of them, and you don't act like one of them. Don't die for people who despise you, Scott!"

"I never had nuthin till I joined up with Danny! You think a man in this city gave a damn about me till dey knew I was part a' Danny's crew? You think anybody ever called me 'Mr. Hanlon' or showed me any respect till den? Huh! Do you!"

"There's a difference between respect and fear, Bull."

"Not for me there ain't! Now shoot if your gonna! I ain't turning on dem! Not now, not ever!" The sirens are closer now; they'll be here in moments! I'm out of time… I un-cock the hammer and lower the pistol.

"He doesn't deserve your loyalty, Scott." I back away slowly, careful not to lose my footing on the frozen rooftop. He doesn't make his move till I'm climbing over the ledge onto the fire escape. He charges into me, talking me like a linebacker over the ledge, we land with a crash on the cold steel of the stairs. He brings all two hundred plus pounds down on top of me and crushes the wind right out of my lungs!

"I ain't letting you kill him neither!" He wraps his ham hock fists around my throat and squeezes! He's strong; too strong…my world starts to swim as my sight starts to go black. I do the only think I can think of and jam a thumb into his left eye! He howls like a wounded beast, letting go of my neck and clutching at his eye with both hands! I kick as hard as I can and send him tumbling off me! I'm gasping for air, my chest aching, my throat burning as I struggle to choke down ragged breaths. He's on me before I can recover, kicking me in the ribs over and over! He tries to bring his foot down on my throat but I manage to catch it and twist hard, he spins and crashes into the railing. Hands flailing for purchase he tumbles off the fire escape and into the night. He shrieks as he falls and lands with sickening thud. I can't bring myself to look.

I can see his girl leaning out the window; she's dressed now and waving at me frantically. I make my way coughing and gasping down to her window and slump inside.

"The lummox, he is dead?" I nod, to busy trying to fill my lungs to be shocked by her accent. "I will, how you say 'Make things square' with police. You, get rid of coat and hat." I hear the police at the ruins of her front door, she disappears into the front room as I ditch my hat and coat beneath her bed. She's a masterful actress whoever she is. She puts together quite the sale of the notorious mobster Bull Hanlon breaking into her home in a jealous rage and nearly killing her new boyfriend. He then apparently slipped and fell to his death on the ice-slicked fire escape while fleeing from the police.

The cops take one look at my rapidly bruising throat and buy every syllable. They know Bull and who he worked for. I don't have to say a thing, I barely can. She glances back at me as the cops take her statement; all I can do is nod my thanks. In the movies this is a heroic win, the vicious gangster meets his just end and our hero lives to fight another day. But this isn't a movie and Hollywood is full of liars. Bull wasn't that bad a man, and I'm sure as hell no hero. I glance up again at the woman who just saved me from the chair and I can't help but wonder what this is going to cost me.

22. White Russian

I'm used to dealing with gangsters. I grew up with them, I've spent my whole life around them. These guys, these Russians, are a very different breed. I had always heard that they're a patient people, not this bunch. It didn't take long for them to call in the favor I found myself owing.

Vito Candolini is a man of the people; he believes that people should have what they want, when they want, no matter what Johnny Law has to say about it. People fear him; you don't get called "The Shark" because you're the humanitarian of the year, but just as many respect him. Some even love him, in an odd sort of way. Danny Doyle is a thug and a maniac, all he has ever cared about is lining his pockets and doing whatever pops into that twisted brain of his. I don't know if his own mother loves him but I'm damn sure she's afraid of him. This guy, I don't know what the hell to make of him.

He works fast, if nothing else. I'm in a car and on my way south to Fulton less than twenty-four hours after my run in with Bull. Two granite faced goons flank me in the back seat of one the finest cars I've ever been abducted in. The Rolls Royce speaks volumes about my new friends. Lyudmila sits up front with the driver, she turns to check up on me and reassure me that all is well every few minutes. That helps less than she thinks. We pull up to one of the most ridiculous looking little restaurants I've ever seen. The walls are red and green striped and the roof shining gold. It takes me a second before I realize it's decorated like the Kremlin. It feels absurdly out of place in the new anti-communist America. We all pile out of the car and my guards motion for me to enter.

Viktor Andreiovich Romanov is as massive and imposing a figure as you'd want in a gang lord, made all the more intimidating by the long scar down the left half of his face. Topping the whole impression of barely contained malice is his one milky white eye, rendered useless in the incident that gave him the scar. He's also the hairiest man I've ever seen, grey from his head down the pelt on his knuckles. He pours each of us a glass of strong smelling vodka as his grim henchmen look on.

"You are no doubt surprised to find us here, da?"

"I didn't think there were many Russians out here." I get a good whiff of the Vodka, I'm not sure I'm interested.

"We are White Russians. You are familiar with the term?" Viktor takes a long easy swig from his glass. I'm still not sure I'm interested.

"You fought for Czar Nicholas during the Bolshevik revolution."

"Oh ho! A scholar we have here! He was distant cousin and simply the 'fall guy' I believe is the term. Damn those Marxist bastards to hell!" He knocks back the rest of his drink and begins to pour another. "You are wondering why I have brought you here."

"I was curious." I take a pull from the vodka. It's eye opening.

"Your Don Vito has gone 'down the river' is it?"

"Up the river."

"Ah, of course, yes. With his going up the river there will be certain needs in your city, needs that my associates and I can meet most readily! There is of course the problem with Mr. Doyle, but it seems you are already 'On the case'! When Lyudmila told me who it was she had encountered, I could not believe the luck! You are exactly the man we are in most need of!" He ends with what I'm guessing is meant to be a reassuring grin. It brings to mind being mauled by a grizzly.

"I'll save the 'thank you' until you finish." I consider taking another pull of the Vodka, but think better of it.

"Ho ho! A wise man indeed! You are already eliminating our competitors, for that you have my thanks!" He raises his glass to me, I return the gesture. "Also though, you know people, contacts of Don Vito's that we need to do business in your city. You will take my Lyudmila, and you will make introductions to these people. She is face of our organization, for mine is not so pretty as hers!" He waves his hand over the massive scar and laughs loudly. His men share the joke with him and all have a good laugh. It's the first sign of life I've seen out of them since I got here. I just smirk and nod my head.

"That's easy enough. A lot of them aren't going to like it much, but how many of us have a choice right now?" Viktor laughs again, long and loud, rumbling like thunder across the empty restaurant.

"You are a man of my own heart! A pragmatist! There is one more thing, then, we will consider your debt paid, for now. I am lover of your American music, The Jazz most especially. It would be an honor if you would favor us with a song." I sit up straight, eyes widening. This just became a lot more uncomfortable.

"You know more than you let on Viktor."

"Da, always. It is how I am alive and my poor idiot cousin is not." I nod, and make my way across the small restaurant to the upright piano in the corner. I ease myself onto the bench next to Lyudmila. She looks a lot more like a giddy child than a mobster's daughter. No one has looked at me like that in a long time.

"Anything specific you'd like to hear?" My fingers reach and flex, testing the old piano. It plays surprisingly well; they've kept it well tuned if nothing else.

"I have always enjoyed your 'Blue Sundays' tune. It is favorite of my Lyudmila as well." She nods eagerly.

I haven't played in over a year now, I haven't even thought about trying. I look at my hands with their knuckles scarred and calloused. They aren't a musician's hands anymore. I feel the ache from countless punches, the creaking of battered bones. I stretch them out; they're stiff from the cold. It doesn't take long for them to remember what they once were, and they don't mind forgetting what they've become.

23. A Long Evening

I duck a haymaker that whistles over my head and clips the top of my hat, knocking it off into the gray snow. I lunge in with a left, Darwin drops his elbow down and I get a fistful of bone. The impact rings through my arm in the cold, but I know his is hurting more. Darwin Finn steps back, shaking his right arm. Good, that one counted.

Delilah is covering him with her .45, she told me she was coming with me tonight, and in Delilah fashion refused to take no for an answer. Darwin Finn is a small fish, but he knows where Patty is. Unfortunately, he also knows I want him alive.

"Oh, just let me shoot him once or twice! I'm tired of watching you two dance, it's dreadfully boring!" I'm about to say something when I catch a face full of dirty snow. Something large barrels into me and knocks me sprawling! A weight crashes down on my chest and I barely get my arms up in time to stop the blows raining down on me. I grab blindly until I feel my hands close on a thick wrist, and then I yank as hard as I can and roll to my right, dislodging Darwin and buying myself time to wipe my face clear. I'm up and on my feet, but he's up quicker and already charging.

Darwin's a small fish but he's a damn tough small fish. Dee's right, it'd be easier to shoot him but that puts me no closer to Patty O'Shaughnessy. He's in mid bull rush when he slips on the frozen concrete, I bring my knee up hard into his breadbasket! He lets out a groan as the air vacates his lungs and he collapses to his hands and knees, gasping in the filthy snow of the secluded back alley.

"I don't like her."

I'm about to launch a kick into Darwin's ribs but I pause in mid strike.

"Wait, what? What are you talking about?"

"That Russian tart you've been tomcatting around with! I don't like her one bit! I see how she fawns over you!" Is this actually happening to me?

"Dee, we gotta do this now?" Darwin kicks out at my left leg and I feel is buckle under me. Over I go once again. This time Darwin turns to run, but I just manage to flail out an arm and trip him up once again. I am already tired of this fight. Darwin is up, quick as a cat and coming at me again! He launches another vicious right but this time I'm ready. I grab his wrist with my left hand, turn into his arm and smash my right elbow into his nose with the full force of his charge and all my bodyweight behind it! His eyes roll up in his head over the wreck that was his nose and he falls straight back as soon as I let go of his wrist. Bill taught me that trick; apparently he learned it from his time in Japan. They don't fight fair over there.

"Well why didn't you just do that to start with? You'd think you weren't trying to win! The way you dilly-dally, honestly!" She slips the .45 back into her new fur coat. I think it's new, it's not the one she had on the last time I saw her.

"It gets easier if someone doesn't keep distracting me." I retrieve my hat and brush the grey snow off of it. "Or God forbid you could have actually helped me."

"And ruin my new mink? You are a crazy one, darling! I did offer to shoot him!" She shrugs at me and gives me that, Oh well, what can you do, look. "You're getting off topic. I don't like her one bit!"

"Well, in her defense" I groan as I hoist the unconscious Finn up to his feet. He's a big boy and hauling him to the car so we can take him someplace private won't be easy. "She actually saved my life recently, unlike some other ladies I might name. Could you at least give me a hand hauling this guy?"

"New mink!" she exclaims, favoring me with a look that proclaims me the single most foolish man on the planet. "We've been over this a dozen times, none of that counts! I simply cannot fathom why you insist on bringing that up over and over!"

"Sure, ok, that's fine." I drag Darwin out of the alley; the street is deserted thank God. "For one thing, it was hardly tomcatting; I owed her family a favor since she very kindly kept a murder rap off my back."

"Oh, he's going to bleed all over my upholstery!" Delilah has got the back door to her new sedan open for me as I slide Darwin's unconscious form in.

"I told you to bring the plastic sheeting." I finish shoving Darwin into the sedan and slam the door shut.

"If you weren't so sloppy we wouldn't have needed it!" We both get in and she turns the engine over. "I've seen you fight before, you're usually much better than that! I bet if your new Russian girlfriend were here you'd have put on a much better show!"

"Just drive Dee." I pull my hat down low over my eyes. This is going to be a long evening.

24. Monkey Bars and Kangaroo Courts

The Mayor is all over the front pages of The Times again. Grinning his idiot grin and promising that a new day has dawned for our fair city. Vito Candolini is going to trial tomorrow, and they are going to throw the book at him. He's going to the chair, thanks to that god damn traitor nephew of his. Jimmy Knuckles sold him out to save his own hide after he had tried to kill him. Well, tried to kill us, but I just happened to be in the room and he sure as hell wouldn't have been sorry if I had been gunned down as well. So there stands our beloved mayor, on the steps of city hall, promising a new safer future now that the Candolini mob will soon be a thing of the past. The best part, the one that makes me smile, is at the very end.

"When asked about the recent rash of slayings of men reputed to be connected with Doyle Gang the Mayor replied 'No Comment'. When he was pressed further on the issue the Mayor declared the press conference over and thanked the reporters present for our time. There has been no official word on who is behind the killing spree that has left over a dozen of the Doyle Gang's men dead, but a source within the MPD, speaking on the condition of anonymity, has stated that they are presently pursuing unaccounted for members of the Candolini Mob. As many readers will recall only a few short months ago open warfare erupted between the Candolini Mob and the Doyle Gang…." He goes on for another paragraph, but it's nothing I don't already know.

I wave my empty glass at the barkeep, who meanders over and fills it up with two fingers of glorious brown medication. This has not been a red letter day for me. I'm about 99% sure I got made by Four Fingers Mallory. I need to do something about him. I recall very clearly giving him one opportunity to get out of my city. Some people never listen. So here I sit, feeling entirely too conspicuous, trying to decide what I'm going to do about the four Doyle gangsters at the table in the far corner. The smart part of me, the part that wants to live to see tomorrow, says walk away. It tells me to pay my tab, pull my hat low and excuse myself as quietly as I can. The only issue, the one glaring problem, is at that same table sits Jacky McNeely. He's on the list, and he needs to die.

I feel the reassuring weight of my .38, hanging close to my heart, and begin to weigh my options. The bar is half full of well-dressed and largely innocent bystanders. If lead starts flying more than a few of them are going to get caught in the crossfire, I'm not okay with that. Four Fingers knows I'm here, so no way to catch them off guard. If I make a move towards that table I'm dead. If I try to wait till they get out front it'll be a four on one ambush, well, three on one. Peter is generally not much good in a gunfight. He proved that the day I shot off his finger. I think I might just be fucked. I'm about to wave the barkeep back over, when an all too familiar four fingered hand alights on the bar to my left.

"Mr. Mallory, I'm quite surprised to see you. I had heard you'd left town." I keep my voice as low and dry as I can manage. He slides me another whiskey with his maimed appendage.

"Ah, well ya' see certain business concerns arose and I simply couldn't get away! Tryin' ta' get a day off from me boss is murder." He chuckles. We both know it's closer to true than he'd like. "I've however been tryin' ta represent yer interests within the organization."

"I noticed. I had a little talk with the late Mr. Hanlon, he mentioned you a few times." I slam home the whiskey, feeling the warmth spread through still cold limbs.

"Poor, stupid bastard. I told him not ta get mixed up with that Russian tart. Scotty was a good lad, but he never had much sense."

"If I recall correctly, I believe I mentioned I'd be terminating our arrangement if you continued to do business in my city." I'm trying to keep my voice low, trying to be calm, but the booze, the thought of still being in debt to the Russians and the sheer fact that one Jacky fucking McNeely is twenty feet away and still breathing are making it God damn difficult!

"I'd hoped ya' reconsider, if I offered ya a wee gift a' good faith. The lads and I are about to escort Mr. McNeely out, and if ya' happen to be lurkin' about, well we'd not bother ya in the least." Peter tilts back a final shot and turns without another word. As good as his word all four men, gather up coats and hats and begin to bundle up. I lay a twenty on the bar and make my exit. The snow hasn't stopped, and in a moment I'm chilled to the bone. This winter feels like it'll never end, I'm starting to forget what the sun looks like. Thankfully, they don't keep me waiting. Peter and his goons are the first ones out the door. Peter looks me square in the eye, and steps aside as Jacky McNeely exits the bar.

Jacky McNeely is still pulling his hat on when he looks up to see the business end of my .38. It takes him just a moment to realize what's just happened.

"Ah yeh' fucking bast……" he doesn't get to finish the thought.

25. Far From Home

"You always take me to nicest places." We haven't even been in The Deuce for ten seconds before Delilah starts in on me.

"First off, I didn't take you anywhere. I said I was going, you decided to come. Second, feel free to go home. No one handcuffed you to the table."

"Not yet, but the night is young!" She smiles at me and waves the waitress over. The Deuce is quiet tonight, with nothing but the usuals having braved the snow and ice. It's coming down like all hell outside and I'm just glad to be indoors for a while. Delilah orders us a bottle of Whiskey and a beer apiece. I have a few moments of blissful silence while we wait for our order and Delilah pours us each a shot. "So why are we here?" and there it goes…

"I'm here because I wanted to sit in my booth, smoke my cigarettes and drink cheap whiskey. You're here because you like making my life difficult." I tap out of a Lucky and offer the pack to Delilah. She takes one and affixes it to her ridiculous cigarette holder. I light hers first before taking the Zippo to my own. The black lighter as served me well for years, another gift from Uncle Sam, one of the few I've still got.

"You sad, silly man. I'm here to add color to your life, and add a bit of fabulous to this dreary place. Though the waitress is quite lovely, I can almost understand why you come here so often." She gives me another wink.

"I wouldn't say that so loud, that's Franklin's daughter and he keeps a shotgun under the bar. Don't get any fresh ideas." I down my shot and chase with a slow pull from the beer, it's exactly what I need right now.

"You are terrible!" Delilah does her shot and makes a sour face "And so is this!" She takes several swallows of her beer. "And that didn't help. What is wrong with you?" Now that makes me smile. I pour another shot for myself and offer Dee the bottle, she politely declines.

"Sorry it's not up to your usual standards. I recall we've had this problem before." I briefly reflect on the second time Dee and I met, when she had me at gunpoint, straight out of the shower no less. Not one of my most shining moments, I'll admit.

"Yes we did, and you promised you'd do better. Will you never stop disappointing me?" she puffs away, adding to the haze that permeates The Deuce, the thick smoky cloud that feels so much like home.

"God, I truly hope not." I can tell she wants to throw something at me, but thinks better of it at the last second. She's off her game tonight; I can't normally get under her skin this easily. It took me till now to notice but she definitely looks anxious. This can't be good. "What's wrong with you tonight?"

"Whatever do mean?" She keeps glancing at the door…

"Dee." She turns and smiles and really does try her best to look perfectly innocent. I can feel the hair on the back of my neck rise.

"Well, as I'm sure you recall, I've recently returned from a trip overseas, somewhat earlier than expected…"

"What did you do?" I'm trying to keep calm, but I've got a very bad feeling about where this is going.

"It was just such a trivial thing really…"

"What did you *DO?*" The door to the deuce opens wide, sucking out some of the smoke and letting in a fresh blast of snow and freezing night air. A few of the barflies up front grumble at the newcomer to shut the door and he eventually does. It's about then I notice he's making a b-line straight for us. "God damn it, Delilah…" I shoot her an angry look as our new friend makes his way to the table. He doesn't look any different from any other poor idiot in from the cold, but he's carrying himself in a way that screams trouble.

"Pardon mate, need a moment wit' your bird there." Hmm, he's a Brit, that's new.

"Hey friend, why don't you pull up a chair, have a shot on me." I pour out a shot and slide it across the table to him. He ignores it, glaring intently at Delilah.

"Sorry 'friend', I'm in a bit of a rush. Another time."

"Really, it's coming down pretty bad out there; it's not safe to be out in that mess. Please, have a seat, join us for a drink and warm up a little."

"I apologize if I was making myself unclear." He slams a revolver onto the table, a Webley .455. Don't see many of those this side of the Atlantic. "I was not making a polite request."

"That was a mistake." The sound of a dozen or so hammers being cocked and the resounding chick-chack of a twelve gauge being racked break the quiet. He turns his head slowly to see more than few .45s, one pump action shot gun and even a captured German Walther pointed at his back. "Now the way I see it, you have three options. You can put the gun away, sit down and have a drink and we can talk like civilized folk do. You can turn around and walk out that door and we can discuss things there, or you can die where you're standing. Personally, and this is just my preference, I'd rather drink than fight tonight. Now put it away, slowly." He does what I tell him and very slowly puts the pistol away. One by one the rest of the bar goes back about its business and a few moments later it's like nothing ever happened. "Have a seat and have a drink." He does. "Now can we be reasonable people here?"

"Look mate, she made off wit' something belonging to my employer, a thing of great value to him and I simply cannot return empty handed." I offer our guest my pack and he lights up eagerly.

"Sounds like a simple enough solution." I look over to Delilah, who smiles sheepishly and pours herself a shot. "or maybe not then. Okay, we can settle this up then and no one needs to get hurt. What did she take?"

"A cross sir, golden with silver filigree and a ruby in the center. One of the very few things my good master managed to save from The Blitz. Been in the family more than 300 years I'm told."

"And you sold it didn't you?"

"Well…" Delilah gives me a shrug and reaches for the bottle again.

"Okay, here's what we can do. I know something like that can't be paid for. We'll get it back for you. I'm sure Delilah can get in contact with someone and we'll buy it back. Simple enough."

"Well…" she says again.

"Alright, plan b. I'll give you twice whatever you took for this job to walk away. Say you lost her trail, or she ran to the Orient. I don't care but I'll make it worth your while." I offer him my hand over the table and I can tell the gears are grinding in his head.

"You pay me now, tonight and I may yet be able to forget I was ever here."

"I'm sure we don't have anywhere near that much on us right now, would you be willing to come with us. I'll give you my gun, no tricks, no funny business."

"I'd be willing." He finally takes my hand and good as my word I slide my pistol across the table to him. He takes it and tucks into his belt and we get up to go. Franklin gives me a look as we gather our coats and hats and I give him a nod. Everything's fine. The cold bites hard as soon as we set foot into the night. The snow's slowed some, but the sidewalks are already covered. It's a god awful night for a walk. We're not half a block from The Deuce when the inevitable happens; I hear the cock of a hammer from behind. The Brit has my .38 out and pointed at my back.

"You don't have to do this you know."

"Sorry mate, I really am. You seem a good sort, but naught but blood will satisfy my master." He raises the gun to the back of my head and I flinch as a shot rings out. Much to my surprise I seem to lacking a hole in the head. Our British friend however, is not so fortunate. Still smoking in Dee's gloved hand is a pearl handled .380 pocket automatic. Should have figured she'd have at least one purse gun.

"Well that's two surprises tonight." I take my gun back from the dead man's hand. Seems a shame he came all the way here to end up like this. Poor idiot, poor damn fool got himself killed for nothing. Reminds me of someone I know. Am I really so different? I have to tell myself I am, or I don't think I could face another day. I can't tell if Dee is shaking from the cold or nerves. I take her hand and we leave another mistake behind.

26. Still Alive

Sometimes, just sometimes mind you, all I want out of life is a quiet evening someplace dark and smoky. Someplace where the whiskey is decent and no one gives a good god damn about making conversation with me. To be just another faceless man in a rumpled suit who's had a long day. I don't think that's asking for too much. Tonight, it seems like pure extravagance.

I don't know how it happened, I don't know how drunk I must have been, but somehow Delilah talked me into coming along to one of her "Society Functions". She seemed convinced I owed her one, though I seem to recall it differently. I don't know which one of her ex-husbands club's this is, but I wish to God I was elsewhere. For now I've managed to sneak out onto a balcony for a smoke and some silence.

"There you are!" Well, at least I still have the smoke. I turn from the rather impressive view of the city. Delilah is dressed in all her newest and finest. For someone with ten grand worth of price on her head, she seems terribly unconcerned. "You, Mister, are supposed to be in here playing nice." She smiles and her emerald eyes shine. I think the more uncomfortable I am the more she enjoys it.

"This isn't really my crowd, Dee." I turn back to face the night, it's as clear as it gets here in winter. I can almost make out the moon through the thick layer of gloom that hangs over my city. It may not snow tonight, that'd be a welcome change.

"Oh you're right! No one here has shot at you all night!" She's beside me now and laughing in my ear. "Whatever will you do? Why..." she glances over her shoulder "there's not a single gangster around!"

"You know that's not what I mean; I've never been comfortable around that much money." I slip another Lucky out my pack before offering one to Delilah. She produces a slender black cigarette holder from somewhere unseen and curtseys her thanks. It's a move so ridiculous I can't help but smile. My Zippo flashes to life as I see to both our cigarettes.

"You are a very silly man. I know how much you still have in the bank; how you, of all people, could say you're uncomfortable with money is just beyond me!" She takes a deep inhale and blows out a perfect smoke ring. It hangs in the dim light for a moment before the breeze sweeps it away.

"It's not the cash, it's the attitude. I've seen up more noses tonight than a doctor during flu season." She tries to stifle a snort, smoke coming out her nose. "Which ex husband of yours was a member here? Number three was it?"

"Number two actually! Dear old Harold, God rest his soul." She very nearly makes me believe that was sincere.

"You are the kiss of death Delilah." I shake my head as she feigns indignation.

"I kissed you, and you're still alive!"

"The only reason I am is plain dumb luck, you've nearly gotten me killed four times already! You took money to kill me, twice! TWICE!"

"In all fairness darling, I only lured you to your death the first time. Danny didn't actually pay me to murder you until the second time which, as you know, I most certainly did not! Now he wants me dead almost as badly as he does you! You show such little appreciation for that! I thought you had better manners!"

For a second I just stare at her, I can't tell if she's serious or not. I can never tell with Delilah. Half the time I think she must be completely insane, the rest of the time I'm sure I'm the crazy one, as I keep putting up with it.

"Thank you for not murdering me, while I was buck naked and fresh out of the shower. I really appreciate you not gunning me down for pay."

"Aaaaannnnnnnnddddd…" she looks at me, expectantly.

"And for getting yourself on Danny Doyle's hit list?"

"See! How hard was that?" She laughs and it makes her eyes sparkle in a most distracting way. "You're entirely welcome by the way! I never did care for that little troll Doyle."

"Then why did you work for him?" I try to match her smoke ring, and as usual it doesn't quite shape up.

"He pays very well; a woman has her needs after all! I mean, do you know how much it costs to look this fabulous all the time?" She twirls and gives me a good look at all of her. I can't even imagine how much she spent on this outfit.

"Not to mention replace all those cars that keep getting shot up."

"Yes yes, that too. I should start charging you for those, as they are entirely your fault! A good deed never goes unpunished!" She sighs and moves in next to me, leaning on the rail of balcony. "I suffer so much for you and what do you do when I try to get you to have a little fun? You skulk around in the shadows and complain, complain, complain! Oh, I'm so sad, I have to eat decent food for a change and spend a night not trying to get myself killed! Boo hoo hoo!" She rubs her eyes like a child crying over a broken toy, the sheer silliness of it keeps from getting as mad as I'd like to be.

"You know why I'm doing this Dee, that bastard Doyle stole everything that ever mattered to me." I'm trying not to yell, my voice is cold and flat. "I'm sorry I'm not always smiles and sunshine Dee. I've buried to many people I love, I just don't have it in me."

"But you're still alive, you have a choice! You can make a new life, a good life, someplace far away from this hell hole! Someplace with me…" her voice goes quiet and soft and for the first time since I met her I know for dead certain she's not joking. "Let's go…please let's just go…"

"Dee, I can't…" she looks at me, eyes wet and hurt and angry.

"No, I don't know why I thought you could. Maybe I thought you were still alive, but you aren't, are you?" She spins on her heel and is on her way back into the party before I can pry my lips apart.

I want to say something, I want to tell her she's wrong, I want her to tell her I don't want to bury her too, but I don't. The heavy curtains close behind her and I'm left on my own.

27. One Man Band

Life has a way of sending me clarity when I need it most. I'm back at the Deuce of Clubs, because honestly where else would I go? The music is bad, the beer is terrible and the place reeks of smoke, failure and loss. It's good to be home. The Deuce is busy tonight, the unrelenting winter eased up just enough to let a man get out of the house for a few hours. It's as much as relief for the rest of the patrons as it is for me. We all have our demons, and there's nothing worse than being locked up with them all damn winter. It'll make you do crazy things.

I'm so wrapped up in my own little universe that I don't even notice Franklin hobbling over until he drops into the seat across from me. He's dressed the same as always, starched white shirt, black bowtie and apron; he's the best dressed man in the room. It's his place though, so who's gonna say boo about it?

"How's the leg?"

"The one I got or the one I ain't?" He smiles and his pearly whites contrast starkly against his dark skin. "The one I got is alright, the other one you got to ask the Nazis about." Franklin, like so many others, left a piece of himself on some battlefield back in Europe. "This ol' wooden piece of shit ain't worth whatever the army paid fo' it, that's for sure."

"I think this is the first time I've seen you leave the bar." I offer him my pack of Luckys but he waves them off. "You feeling alright?"

"Suzie and Caroline got it alright back there. Better question is, what the hell you doing back here? That Doyle fucker's got one of his assholes here every damn night looking for you, after the shit you pulled with that Limey." Franklin leans down, adjusting his wooden leg. I can hear a soft "Motherfucker" just under the music.

"I know, there's a car full of them out front." I take a long pull of the beer, it's even worse warm.

"The hell you doin' you crazy honkey? Tryin' to get an ol' man killed?"

"Nope, they don't have the nerve to come in here and start anything. This place of full of a lot of drunk, angry vets with guns; it'd be suicide. So they're going to sit out there in cold while I stay here, stay warm and listen to yet another of Millburgh's most horrendous bands. I swear to God Franklin I don't know where you find these guys."

"What I gots ta' pay, you cain't get the best. You wanna go play fo free you welcome to!"

"Maybe next time."

"Always next time wit you! You gonna do something about them assholes outside?" Franklin groans as he rises on his one good leg.

"Absolutely. Once they're tired, frozen and figuring I'm blind drunk, I'm going walk out there and shoot every one of them."

"Well don't go and get yoself killed, you a good tipper." With another brilliant grin Franklin ambles back across the bar in the odd rolling gait of the one legged man. I light up a fresh smoke and suck down a lung full of warmth. I don't know how man survived before these things. I lean back in my booth and watch the band struggle through their set. It's painful to watch, but most of the room is ignoring them anyhow. I let my eyes wander around the Deuce as I get reacquainted with the old girl.

There's a sea of faces in the Deuce, most of them I've seen a hundred times before. The walls are covered in pictures, nearly every one of soldiers. Franklin came back from the war a little earlier than most, having the misfortune to be a bit closer to an exploding shell that the surgeon general advised. When others starting trickling home he welcomed one and all into the Deuce. Didn't matter who or what you were before the war, if you've seen the elephant you're welcome to drink at the Deuce. I think Franklin only let me stick around for the novelty of it, until I became just another face in the crowd. Eventually he even quit asking me to play the battered old upright piano, which even still sits lonely and untouched in the far corner. Well, he quit asking so often. I didn't want to call any more attention to myself than I need to, there's comfort in being just another face.

I once asked Franklin, years ago, why he called the place The Deuce of Clubs. "Lowest card in the deck Boss, lowest card in the deck." was all he said. I'm ashamed to admit it took me a while to figure out what he meant. The place has always had an air of hard luck and hard living, from the warped bar, to the peeling wallpaper, to the uneven stage, to the sullen eyed patrons speaking low and trying to forget the toils of their day and the ghosts that haunt them. It's the greatest and most terrible place I've ever been, and I never want to leave. After a few hours of nursing my drinks Franklin rings last call. I check my pistol and don my hat and coat. I give my fellow patrons a moment to clear out, no sense in getting any of them shot. With a final nod to Franklin I stagger out into the night.

I slip and stumble on the icy sidewalk, barely catching myself on the wall of the Deuce. I've got to really sell this, and I'm doing my damndest. I slip and slide a few more feet before I let my legs go out from under me and crash into a laughing heap in the snow and ice.

"Need a hand there?" I turn my head slowly, and look squinting and shaky at the four men who've appeared behind me. They could at least try to be subtle about this. They could have shot from me the car, but I'm willing to bet Danny would hand out hundreds like candy if they brought me to him alive.

"I sheem to have fallen over…."I lay it on thick, and their

knowing grins tell me I have them sold.

"Well then laddie, let me give ya a hand there!" He bends down reaching for my left arm. I let him help me start to rise before I me weight goes dead and I drag him back down, landing in a heap. He yells clutching at his guts as the red begins to pool in the snow. It takes his boys a second to realize what's happened, but it's already too late. One, two, three shots rip the stillness of the night. Mr. Helpful is still screaming, hands clutching at the knife buried to the hilt in his gut. He writhes and twitches, churning the snow into a nightmarish pink mess. I put one in his brain and give the night back to silence.

28. The Deep Dark

Have I ever mentioned that I hate boats? Well, not so much boats, but the inky-black death that lingers just beneath their all-too-fragile hulls. My home has always been a nautical town, and the harbor kept us afloat through a lot of the lean years. The sea helped make this city what it is, and she has demanded more than her pound of flesh. We grew up with it, expected it, it is just how it is here. When the war came nearly everyone who served became a sailor or a marine. I read the hometown paper all through the war, read the stories of all the poor bastards who went down into the deep dark. Local sons sacrificed to blue demon. "No thank you!" said I, not interested! So why then am I am sneaking onto this old Liberty Ship? That's a fair question.

Earlier tonight, my new Slavic friends sent me a gift, a thank you present for introducing them to a few of the less ethical types around town. Lyudmila had come by with two things, the name of this ship and a time. She wouldn't elaborate on anything else, but it didn't take me long to figure out who would be waiting. Someone has been through here before me, that much is clear. There's a conspicuous lack of the armed men I spotted, huddled against the cold that are posted round the rest of the vessel. The knotted rope hanging from the deck doesn't much hurt either. So I climb, it's not easy, the rope is slick, but not frozen. It couldn't have been here long.

I take my time, climbing as slowly as I can, trying to keep the swinging of the rope to a minimum. No one has seen me yet, but no one gets this lucky for long. Just to prove my point I spot a face peering down over the railing directly above. I'm nearly two-thirds of the way up, no choice now. I go for my gun, but he's waving his hands and making the "shush" motion at me. Without any other option I holster my pistol and resume the climb. He extends his hand at the top and pulls me over the rail.

"You must be silent." His whisper is low and harsh, his

English deeply accented. "Follow the deck through that bulkhead. The way is clear. Boris sends his gratitude, and wishes you luck." I can't get a good look at him, his face is painted black and he's off and over the side before I can even thank him for the assist. I move on, staying low and quiet. I am intensely thankful that the harbor has frozen up enough to hold this behemoth steady. I'm not sure how quiet I can be on a rolling deck. I nearly stumble over the first of the bodies. His throat neatly cut, his blood still steaming in the frozen air. That poor bastard never saw what hit him, and he's not alone. I come across three more, similarly dispatched, before I make my way into the darkness of the open bulkhead. The man who took these lives was ruthless, quick and utterly professional. I hope I never see him again.

It's near pitch black inside the ship, and I have no idea where I'm going. I make my way forward slowly, inching along, one hand on the wall to my left. A few more steps in and I hear it, faintly, but clearly, music, Violin music? Using the sound as a guide I move forward, until I see the faintest glow of light ahead. Someone has left a bulkhead open just a crack, just enough to let a flicker of light and the sound of music trickle out into the dark. I draw my weapon and make my way as quietly as I can to the door. Whoever is playing is a virtuoso, the sound is beautiful beyond reason. I want to sit and listen, but I recall why I'm here and there's no time for that. The music stops abruptly as I reach the door. The hell with, I kick at it hard and bound in gun raised!

There stands Patty O'Shaughnessy, violin in hand, looking as imperturbable as always. He glances at the gun, the looks me in the eye. I meet his bespectacled gaze.

"I didn't think you had it in you, Patrick." I motion to the violin.

"The Almighty gives every man his gifts. May I?" He looks to the open case at his feet.

"Slowly." He complies, placing the violin and bow carefully into the case, then locking the lid. "For a second there Patrick, I almost believed you were a human being." He shrugs slightly, the most emotion I've ever seen him show.

"You and I, we aren't all that different."

"I don't murder pregnant women and old men!"

"Ya fill graves, ya make widows and ya break mother's hearts. I don't think old Mrs. Hanlon has stopped weeping for her poor idiot boy. Wasn't my hand on the gun that killed your wife, nor was it mine that killed the old man. Though it was my word, tis true, that sent those men to kill him. It was you what made it him a target, so yer as guilty as I. Now do yer business and be done with it. I may be no more but the shot will ring this place like a bell and every man above decks and below will have ya. You'll not escape with yer life." He right about more of that than I want to admit, I holster my piece and go for my blade.

Patty is fast. He has the violin case up and swinging in a punishing arc at my head. I get an arm up in time to deflect the blow, but the impact numbs my arm and sends me reeling, my knife falling out of my grasp! He got the case up ready to smash it into my face when I drop straight back, kicking hard! He lets out a shout as foot meets knee, knocking him off balance and tripping him out the door! He stumbles and lands hard on the deck, gut crashing into the violin case forcing the wind from his lungs. Feeling is slowly starting to creep back into my right arm, I grab my knife and turn for him but he's already up again, making for the deck. I'm on him as he makes it into the open air.

He tries to shout, but nothing comes out louder than a rasp, his lungs still struggling for air. I hit him again in guts for good measure! I've got hold of my stiletto, but my right arm is still numb and slow. I drive the blade towards his belly with all the force I can manage but he blocks it easily, grabbing my arm and pulling me past him, throwing me to the frozen deck! I slide on my back on the icy surface until my head crashes into a rail, stopping the skid. Patty is still holding his stomach, fighting for breath as I rise slowly to my feet, my ears ringing. He sends me sprawling again with a knee to the face that has me seeing stars! I feel his hands on my collar hauling me up and shoving me hard into the railing! I grab at him with my left hand, clutching for dear life as he shoves me over the side, my weight pulling him with me as we tumble into the night.

We fall together, and I pull as hard as I can to get him underneath me. We spin for a few brief moments, before I feel the bone jarring impact as we meet the frozen sea. Patty took the worst of it; his breath comes in ragged, wet gasps. I landed almost perfectly on top of him and I'm sure something must be broken. Everything hurts! I have just enough time to be grateful that I'm still mostly in one piece when I hear the most horrible sound of my life. The ice groans then cracks and splits, spilling us into the deep dark.

29. Faith

The cold seeps into my bones, it sinks in deep and grabs hold hard. The blue demon has me, her icicle claws plunge into my heart as she pulls me down, down…down. My aching body drifts until there is nothing but the cold, and it is everywhere. The roaring in my ears dulls and fades, I am left in silence. The quiet darkness draws me further and further in until even thought is impossible. Then there is nothing…

I float in the infinite black, alone in my sea of naught. Not even the cold of the Atlantic reaches me fully now. There is only the black, stretching on into forever. I don't know how long I drift; there is no time. There's only the one terrible, eternal moment, an endless pitch black now with no beginning or end.

"What did ya expect, the Pearly Gates and Saint Peter?" The voice is the first sound I've heard in a millennium, or has it been a few minutes? I'm so confused. It sounds so familiar, but I can't open my eyes to look. "No, not for you. The long dark's all there is for the likes a' you!"

I try to open my mouth, try to speak but nothing comes. All sensation of body is gone. All I feel is the cold, and even that feels like something distant and nearly forgotten, an echo from another life.

"I know what ya'd say, had ya lips to say it. Ya'd tell me how righteous and just ya are! How ya never harmed an innocent man, how ya took the lives of the guilty and the dammed! Sinners and villains all! Oh you're a dirty sneak is what ya are. Murderin' the unwary in the darkness, stabbin' an' shootin' in the night! Yer a coward, yer a killer, yer a monster!"

I am nothing of the kind! I took on an army of armed and dangerous men and I did it on my own! They knew my face, knew I was coming for them! They are the cowards, hiding in the dark places, terrorizing and taking from those too weak and afraid to defend themselves! I know that voice. I'm nearly certain it's mine. I wish I knew where it was coming from…

"So who made you judge and jury? Who gave you the right?" The voice is different now, the accent is gone. It sits on the edge of a memory I can't, quite, reach. "You think you're so damn important that you can do as you please! What makes you better than us?"

I did what no one else would! Not one arrest, not one lead in months, MONTHS! I lay in a bed for weeks waiting, praying, that something would be done. That one day someone would come tell me that they had caught the men who killed Gina, who took my child from me before she ever drew breath! I should let that go? I should let them get away with it! I should let them do it again to some other poor bastard? NO! Not again, NOT EVER AGAIN!

"And where did it get you? Who have you helped?" It's a new vice, softer, feminine and full of sorrow. "Does one head rest easier because of you, even your own? No. You unleashed a crazed beast on the world; you made it far crueler and more unpredictable than ever. Everyone in your life will suffer because of you; everyone will pay for your mistakes. Everyone will pay for your failure, and they will curse your name for generations."

I'm not done yet. I'll finish what I started. Danny Doyle will reap in pain what he sowed in blood. When he's gone every person he's ground under his heel will sleep better at night. Every victim he's robbed, everyone he's terrified into paying him protection, everyone he's ruined to build his tiny empire will know he got what was coming to him. You think they'll curse me? You think they'll hate me? Fine, let them! I'll know, I'll always know, that I did what had to be done.

"And how will ya do that now, boyo? Yer naught but a piece of meat sinkin' in the brine." Another voice, it's so familiar…..why can' I remember? I know him, I've known him for years but why can't I remember? "Yer dead boyo, just like me and the rest o' these poor bastards. Here's where yer tale ends, son. Here's where ya stay. Here, ya can do no more harm."

"No." A new voice, the most familiar and intimate yet. "He doesn't belong, not yet. He's not done." She's angry, angry beyond words. Her rage is the first bit of heat I've felt in a thousand lifetimes. "Now, go! I don't want to see you until you finish the job! You're not welcome here, not welcome with me until it's done." It starts then with a memory. A wife......a child......Gina! Wait! Please!

My heart beats, my blood flows. I taste the salty tang of the sea.

30. Fragile Things

I have so little left of my life. Every picture, every letter, every breadcrumb that we leave on the trail of life that says "We were here!" all turned to ash. I still dream of fire, I can still smell the smoke. What I have left offers me little but the coldest comfort.

I spent weeks in the hospital after the shooting. I only left once during those weeks. They let me attend my wife's funeral, and I was so full of morphine that I can barely remember it. When the doctors finally decided I was well enough to leave, I had already heard how little remained. Vito had seen to it that I had a place to go, and everything was waiting for me, such as it was. One suitcase of clothing that had been in the trunk of the car, the coat and hat I had left in the back seat, and one small and rather smoke stained iron box. Inside were my gun and my knife, both gifts from my Gina. I had forgotten all about them, with the baby coming I had locked them away and never gave them second thought.

The knife she bought me on our honeymoon. She had never been back to the land of her forefathers, and we managed to get to ourselves over to Rome for a week. Thankfully we were there and gone before things got out of hand in Europe. Italy is beautiful country; I know it broke her heart to see is bombed into ruins throughout the war. While we were there she bought me this switchblade. She said a real man needed a proper stiletto, and no husband of hers would be without one, even if he wasn't Italian. I have to admit, it is a thing of beauty. Even after some rough handling and a lot of saltwater as of late. Nothing rusts good steel faster than blood and sea salt. My gun on the other hand, was never much to look at.

A model 1899 Smith & Wesson Military and Police, the very first .38 Special ever made. It's the grandpa of the modern revolver; a half step removed the single action six guns of my Grandpa's day. Remind me to tell you about him sometime, he was a strange character. I have no idea where she had kept it all this time, but she made it clear that it was important to her that I have it. All she would ever say was that she knew how much I loved old things, and when she saw it she thought of me. It took a lot of work to bring it back to life, and almost as much to clean it up again after my recent swim. I honestly can't believe both of them aren't rusting at the bottom of the sea. Guess I Shouldn't complain, got to take the lucky breaks when I get them.

Funny thing about the .38, the army quit using them after the Philippines Uprising. The soldiers complained that it didn't have enough stopping power, they'd unload on man and he just wouldn't fall down. It wasn't long after that the .45 colt 1911 became the standard sidearm for America's military. The 1911 is a fine weapon, and it set the standard for everything that's come after it. The .45acp round is definitely deadlier, but I haven't had too much of a problem with that.

I look down at Johnny Boy Blanton, who's currently in the process of bleeding out on the street. I put one is his guts and he dropped like a sack of bricks. He clutches at the wound in his side as his life slips away onto freshly fallen snow. I'm breathing heavy against my damaged ribs, bastard made me chase him. This is the first time I've been out since my tussle with O'Shaughnessy, and wouldn't you know it, turns out the Doyle Gang thought I was dead. I do love disappointing Danny Doyle; I'll try and make a habit of it.

The Army may have quit on the .38, but it's all I have left of her. I give Johnny Boy a few more moments to say his goodbyes to the world before I put an end to his misery. It doesn't take much to turn out the lights on a life. Humans are fragile things and we are so easily broken.

31. The Worst Part

I've been crippled by grief in ways most people will never experience. I live every moment of my day in a constant state of regret. The quiet moments, the hollows of the day are filled with "what if's" and "if only's". I can't stand it.

Most people, most sane, rational, functional people try to move on when tragedy strikes. They try not to wallow in it. Me, I wrapped myself in a blanket of grief and rage so tight that it crushes the air out of my lungs and makes my vision swim. I'm lucky in a way. My tragedy, the great unfairness that struck my life has a face and a name and I can live for the day when I see it for the final time. Most people don't have that either.

I get closer, day by day, to Danny Doyle. I cross name after name off the list, until someday, someday very soon, he'll be the only one left. Today though, today is another matter.

I duck as I come around the corner, two shots shredding brick where my head would have been. I fire once at the muzzle flash and am richly rewarded by a sharp yell and the sound of steel hitting snow.

"Oh God, Oh Jesus!" Conner Riley clutches his right wrist, blood plumbing through tightly clenched fingers. His pistol lay at his feet, as useless as if it were half way around the world. "Please, ya don't have to do this!"

"You murder my wife, you leave me for dead in my burning home and you want to look me in the eye and tell me I don't have to do this?" I cock the .38 and level at his head.

"I was just there ta rob ya, I swear to Mary Mother O' God I never meant ya any harm! It was Danny what shot ya, Danny who killed yer wife and he what set the place ablaze! Please!" His voice is shrill and panicked, the terror lines his face.

"You think I don't know that? I've heard this all before, every damn word."

"Please, oh Jesus, help me! Please don't do this! I never meant..."

"You could have taken anything you wanted. I would have gladly stood by and let you clean out every last thing I owned. I even swore I wouldn't tell the cops I saw any of your faces. You could have walked away clean!" I press the barrel to his forehead; it's already cooled in the frozen air of the January night. "But that wasn't good enough was it?"

"It was Doyle! Please, we never wanted ta' do harm ta' you and yours!"

"Then why didn't a single one of you say a God damn word! He gunned me down in front my wife and shot her twice the belly just to be sure he got our baby too and NONE of you pieces of trash said a GOD DAMN WORD! There were nine of you and one of him!" I press the barrel hard into his head forcing him back against the alley wall.

"Please, ya can't kill me for being a coward. Please!" His whole body shakes and his knees buckle. He collapses into a begging, sobbing mass in the filthy snow.

"You're a terrible actor Riley. I know what you've done since. You are a coward, true, but you're still a monster." The shaking, sobbing mass at my feet stops moving

"Ah, fuck ya ta' the halls o' hell and back! I nearly had ya!" The cylinder turns, the hammer falls and the lights go forever out on Conner Riley.

"No, you didn't."

I leave Riley in the alley with the other trash. I don't bother cleaning out his wallet or taking his gun. I'm not interested in a dime of the blood money that thing that passed for human has. Whatever vagrant cleans him out before the cops show up is welcome to it. A lot of squatters call this part of town home; it won't be long before someone helps themselves. I take out my pack of Luckies and light up with steady, unwavering hands.

I remember the first time I ever spilled blood, I remember the fear and horror of it. It's not like that anymore. I don't even spare a glance over my shoulder. I stroll down the street as calmly as I would walk to a ballgame on Sunday afternoon. I'm numb, and not just from the cold and the worst part, the worst part is, I don't even mind.

32. Ugly as Sin

I never understood the phrase "Ugly as Sin". Times like this, sin seems unutterably beautiful. I'm surrounded by beauty and all of it for sale. This place used to belong to Vito and the Candolini Mob, but since the law brought the hammer down on The Shark and all his boys Madame LaGrange has taken her operation independent. That is, until the Doyle Gang started sniffing around. So here I am, making introductions once again.

Lyudmila and I are perched on a couch of the finest red velvet I've ever felt. A few of the girls are lingering in the foyer, new faces mostly. Hard times lead to hard choices. We've only been waiting for The Madame for a few minutes and I'm already getting fidgety. I was never too comfortable being here. Lyudmila notices me squirming and nudges me with her elbow.

"That one is pretty, no? This may take some time, you should enjoy yourself." She says with a smile and a wink. I'm about to offer a response when Madame LaGrange appears, saved by the bell.

"Madame LaGrange, thank you so much for agreeing to meet with us." I stand and take her gloved hand, kissing it lightly. I've only met The Madame a few times, but she never seems to change. Everything about her is ageless and perfect. Her long, dark hair hasn't a hint of grey. Her dress is immaculate and the same shade of red as the fine upholstery. She fixes her eyes, so dark as to be nearly black on me and I feel an involuntary shiver.

"I should be thanking you dear boy. Nasty little men those Doyle boys, no class whatsoever. Not like poor dear Vito! Have you heard from him?"

"No, I'm sorry, I haven't. They're not letting him have visitors or much contact with the outside world at all. I heard he's gotten a few letters to his wife." I release her hand and fold my own behind my back.

"Well that's something at least. I never did trust that nephew of his. I told Vito years ago that he was no good at all. He never wanted to hear it 'Blood is Blood' and all that nonsense." She turns her gaze from me, giving Lyudmila an appraising look. "And who is your delightful companion?"

"Madame LaGrange, this is Lyudmila. She represents some 'new friends' who might be able to help you with your situation." Lyudmila steps forward and offers her hand, but Madame LaGrange takes her arm in arm and leads her towards the stairs. I start to follow but The Madame shoots me glance over her shoulder.

"Girl talk, my dear boy, I'm sure you understand. Feel free to make yourself at home. Cyndi, be a darling and take care of our gentleman caller would you?" One of the curious new faces hurries over and takes me by the hand. She's young, maybe twenty, with copper red hair cut into a 1920's style bob and brilliant blue eyes set in the most lily white skin I've ever seen. It takes me a moment to make out the freckles her makeup barely covers. She cocks her head slightly, as if trying to remember something.

"You look real familiar mister, you ever been in here before?" I can't place her accent, but she's definitely not a local.

"Not in quite some time, probably well before your time here." She gives me that quizzical look again but leads me out of the foyer and into the main room. Business looks awfully slow today. The snow storm lashing to cost probably has a lot to do with that. There are several girls lounging about the place, looking as alluring as possible for any potential clients. Most don't pay me any mind, as it seems I'm already occupied. I try very hard not to notice the way Cyndi's deep blue and entirely too short dress swishes and flutters as she walks. She stops abruptly, and turns to look me in the face again.

"This is gonna sound strange mister, but I swear I know you from somewhere….your voice sounds so much like….." Those brilliant blue eyes widen dramatically "Wait a minute! Are you…"

"Before you finish, yes I am." I don't know what to call the sound she made as anything other than a squeak of glee. Her grip on my hand tightens significantly and those blue eyes stay wide in wonder.

"Oh my God! I used to listen to your show every week on the radio! My ma used to buy me your records for Christmas and my birth day! Oh my God!" Cyndi is nearly bouncing now her excitement makes me smile despite myself.

"Well, now you're making me feel old." I grin at her; I haven't had anyone react like this in what feels like a lifetime.

"I'm sorry! It's just I grew up listening to your music and that variety show was amazing! Was that really the president you had on?"

"Ok, now I feel really old. Also, no, he was just an impersonator. Sorry to spoil the magic."

"Will you play a song for us? Please? Please!?!?!" Cyndi tugs at my arm pulling me over to the baby grand piano off to the side of the main room. "Lucy! Move! Don't you know who this is? He's going to play a song for us!" Lucy obliges and I slide onto the black lacquered piano bench. Cyndi stands to my right; hands clasped expectantly, eyes pleading.

"Well, the voice isn't quite what it used to be, but I'd hate to disappoint a fan." I crack my knuckles once and place my hands on the keys. They know the way on their own from there. I do my best to give them all a show, to give her a show.

When Lyudmila comes to find me I'm still playing. Cyndi is on the bench next to me, head on my shoulder. The other girls have gathered around, lounging on couches, some just sitting on the floor. Lyudmila grins at the sight and waits until I finish my song.

"We must go. There is much to do." I slide off the bench and offer Cyndi a hand to help her up as well.

"Well ladies, thanks for listening. It's been a real pleasure." We make our way back into the foyer, Cyndi still clasping my hand. Madame LaGrange is waiting for us by the door.

"Thank you, darling" she leans and kisses me once on each cheek. "I have a feeling things will be looking up rather nicely now." She glances at Cyndi who has yet to relinquish her grip on my hand. "Cynthia, dear, it's time for our guest to go. Though I'm sure he'll drop by again soon." Cyndi does let go, but not before hugging me tightly.

"You're coming back right?" Cyndi asks, giving me that expectant look again.

"I'm sure I'll be around. Take care of yourself." I don and my hat and tip it to The Madame. "Madame, a joy as always." Madame LaGrange gives me an approving nod. Lyudmila and I bundle back up and head out into the cold. Lyudmila elbows me in the arm again as we leave.

"You are strange man."

"What?" I open the door to the car for her as she enters as gracefully as one can with so many layers on. Then move around and plop down into the driver's seat.

"You could have had any one of those woman, but instead you are choosing to play piano and put on show. You make no sense." She hits me in the arm again. "Strange man!" The car sputters to life and I pull onto the icy road. I've got nothing to say for myself really, at least nothing that would make any sense to her, so I let the subject die. It was nice to feel like human being again, to remember what life was like. It's good to go back, if only for a moment.

33. A Good Cop

Part of the sorry reality of living in this delightful metropolis is dealing with the fact that those paid to serve and protect, don't often do much of either. It all starts at the top. The Mayor is an empty suit, better at making impassioned speeches and getting re-elected than at any act of administration. The press loves him though, as he's great for a quote and looks good on the front page. I'm not sure if there's any real malice in him, or if he's just been surrounded by sycophants so long that he's forgotten what the word "No" sounds like. The further down the chain you go, the worse it gets.

The average Millburgh cop does enough to get by, but he's not above taking some "benefits" of the badge. He's basically a decent guy doing a tough job in a city rampant with crime. The average cop isn't much of a problem. There are also the dirty ones, who live in the pockets of the mob or just run their own little private empires throughout the city. They aren't much of problem either, slip them a few greenbacks and they develop a case of selective amnesia pretty swiftly. Then there are the honest ones. The good cops out to keep the citizens safe and see justice done. I have the misfortune of running into one of them tonight, and that's really making things complicated.

"You holster that gun right God damn now! This man is in my custody and he is going downtown, and you try and stop me so help me I'll shoot you." Detective Lieutenant Kyle McNulty is not one to make an idle threat. Unfortunately he's also got Timmy Connelly in custody. Tim and I have some unattended to business to resolve.

"Take me in, I don't care, get me the hell away from this nut job!" Tim is backed against a wall, nothing between him and me but an honest man. Timmy knew what was coming; he arranged this meet to turn himself in. Only reason I knew where he'd be tonight.

"Kyle, I really don't have time for this…" I spare a glance over my shoulder, but the night is still.

"I don't give a good god damn about what you got time for! This man surrendered himself to my custody and he is going to prison where he damn well belongs!" The look in his eye says he is not in the mood to hear my counterpoint. I can't blame him. Under the best of circumstances Detective Lieutenant Kyle McNulty is the bitterest son of a bitch I've ever met. He should be a captain by now and everyone knows it. He never played ball, never kissed the right asses, and never worked the politics like a good drone was supposed to. As a result he's climbed as high as the powers that be are going to let him and he knows it damn well. "Now put the gun down or get shot, either way he's coming with me!" I do what he says, moving extra slow holstering my gun.

McNulty cuffs Timmy quickly and shoves him into the back of his car before he turns to address me again.

"You're lucky I'm in a good mood or I'd take you in too. Don't think for one second that I don't know you're the one been taking out the trash lately. I don't have a lick of evidence to prove it though, or I'd haul you in, good mood or no." I'm about to thank him when I catch a dull glint in the dim light of the streetlights, I have just long enough to haul him down into the snow before the night goes all to hell. A torrent of bullets crashes into McNulty's car, shredding windows, steel and flesh. When the stream of fire dies down there's not a sound from inside the car. I can see shoes running across the snow, there are at least two of them and least one is carrying a Thompson.

"I told you I didn't have time for this." McNulty has his service revolver drawn and is already in a crouch ready to move. My own gun is in my hand as I try and find my footing.

"Soon as he opens up again, you go right I'll go left." I don't even have time to agree before the thug with the Thompson opens fire. I dive out from behind the car as it's torn to pieces by the fat, heavy .45 caliber slugs. The thin steel is shredded behind me as I dive. I turn on impact and fire, my shot catching the gunman high on the shoulder spinning him to his left, the stream of fire stitching the wall behind and above me. I see him take two more in the chest and he goes down. I scan the night but there's no sign of the second thug.

McNulty is up in a hurry half sprinting half sliding across the icy street to kick the Thompson away from the gunman's hand. I can see from here there's nothing to be done for him. Warily I get to my feet, eyes checking every dark corner, but the second man is gone, vanished into the night. The inside of McNulty's car is a nightmare, there's nothing left of Connelly but a red ruin. Danny Doyle does not look kindly upon snitches. One more name off the list, I guess the night's not a total loss.

"Shit, shit!" McNulty is on the opposite side of the car, surveying the damage. "This is well and truly fubar." He reaches in for the radio but the microphone is a shattered wreck, there's at least one more hole I can see through the radio itself.

"Looks like you need to find a pay phone, Detective."

"Not another God damn word from you! I promised him protection; he was ready to roll over on Doyle. We could have brought the whole damn gang down." McNulty seethes, his pistol clenched so tight I'm sure his knuckles must be white beneath his gloves.

"I wouldn't lose any sleep over that. One way or another there won't be a Doyle Gang much longer."

"I don't want to hear it. Just get the fuck out of my sight before I think of a good reason to arrest you." I take him at his word and make my way into the night. There's one last name on my list, and now it's time for Danny Doyle and I to settle up. I can't tell you how much I'm looking forward to seeing him again.

34. Mutineer

No one has seen hide nor hair of Danny Doyle since the hit on Timmy Connelly. I know he's running scared now, and that makes me smile. I've checked every spot I know, but in a city this big there are a lot of places to hide. Hence, here I sit, in the Deuce of Clubs, waiting for news. I know it's just a matter of time now.

The most comforting thing about The Deuce is that it never changes. The beer is always cheap and cold; the room smells like tobacco and the faces are always the same. It's more home than home. The room is quiet tonight, filled with the low murmur of men reminiscing about days past, and a youth lost to the ugliness of war. I'm in too good a mood for that. I make my way from my regular corner to the bar where Franklin is holding court as usual. He's got as many stories as anyone in the room, and the wooden leg to prove it.

"I hear your looking for musicians. How much you paying?" Franklin's eyes get wide for a just a second, before his big, warm grin spreads ear to ear.

"Fo' most folks I pays Fifteen a night. Fo' you boss, make it ten." He chuckles in that gravely rumble of his.

"Five bucks and a bottle of whiskey and you have a deal. None of that stuff you brew in your bathtub either, it tastes like old man."

"You speakin' from experience there boss?" He laughs again as he hands a dark brown bottle across the bar. I make a show of checking the label and the seal before opening it and taking a pull.

"My God! There may be actual alcohol in here, you run out of kerosene?"

"Git on up there and earn yo' keep. You workin' fo' me now!" With a half bow I make my way to the old upright piano near the stage. It's beat up and the black paint is fading and chipped, but I know it's still in tune and she'll do the job for tonight. Franklin switches the microphone on and I pick it up.

"Alright you sorry bastards, I don't have to introduce myself do I?" A chorus of No's answers that question for me. "Okay, sing along if you know this one." I start them off with something upbeat and old, one I know even these sour old drunks will know, by the time I get to the chorus a few of them are actually singing along, by the third verse I've got half the bar with me, by the final chorus I've got them hooked. I play tune after tune, keeping with the up-tempo songs, the ones easiest to get into. It feels good to hear them let loose, to hear the voices of these broken souls sing out. They deserve to have a little fun, they deserve to remember.

I give them all I've got, and by the time I'm done my voice is horse and my breathing is ragged. It's a hell of a lot harder now, what with only one lung that works right. They deserve it though; they earned the best I got. I take my nights pay of whiskey and crash back into my corner booth. There's still plenty of time before last call and plenty of time to enjoy my reward for a job well done. The place feels different now, and I'm enjoying the hell out of it. I'm a third of the way through my bottle when the place goes quiet. I look up to see everyone staring at the door. Two figures have made their way inside; I recognize the first as one of Doyle's goons. Mine isn't the only hand reaching for a gun. A second later I recognize the second man, Four Fingers Mallory.

"Franklin, a round for everybody on me. These gentlemen are here to see me I think. They're not going to cause a problem, are they?" I direct the last part of that sentence to the men by the door.

"We're just here for a friendly word is all." Four fingers speaks up, holding up both hands. His maimed right hand, exposed. I wave them over to my table as Franklin pours for everyone in the house.

"I was wondering when you'd show up." I offer Four Fingers the bottle; he declines with a wave of his hand. He's really moved up in the world, I barely recognize him beneath all his new finery. His suit is immaculate, and clearly well-tailored. His bowler derby looks to be crafted of a kind of felt he never could have afforded before. "Look at you, Four Fingers is making it big."

"Ah, it's just 'Fingers' now if ya please."

"I beg your pardon, Fingers, how can I help you tonight? Your boss send you out to collect my head?" I take another long pull from the bottle. Its warmth fills me inside.

"Ya' should know better n' that. Ya' spared me life when ya' had no cause to, and ya' know I'm grateful. Truly, honestly grateful fer that. I think I've done me part as well, lent you a hand more than once, I have." I pull out my pack of Luckies and again offer it to Fingers and friend. Fingers declines but his muscle accepts. My Zippo has us both lit shortly thereafter.

"I'm not arguing with you, but the point of this visit is?"

"Here's how it is, if I can hand Danny over to ya, do I have yer word you'll not come after me or my boys? Even the ones who may have been shootin' at ya' in the recent past." he leans in close, his voice low.

"Your boys?" it takes me a second to catch on in the warm whiskey haze I'm swimming in. "I get it, I get rid of Doyle and Fingers Mallory becomes the new boss of the Doyle Gang? That about the long and short of it?"

"Aye, ya' have it dead to rights. Except I'd be callin' it the Mallory Mob. Sounds a wee bit better don't ya' think?" He grins wide, teeth white in the dim light of the bar beneath is red mustache. "Do I have yer word?"

"Yeah, yeah you do, Peter. Once Doyle is dead I could give a good God damn what the rest of you do." Fingers offers me his good left hand and I clasp it and shake. He takes a small slip of paper out from his coat and slides it across the table to me. "Be there tomorrow night, ten o'clock. Doyle will be there, sure as I live and breathe."

"Till tomorrow then." Fingers and his goon stand, and with a smile and a tip of the cap they're gone. I lean back and contemplate taking another drag off my bottle, but I think better of it. Tomorrow is going to be a busy day.

35. Last Rites

I've been waiting for this day for so long, and now that it's here I've still got a few loose ends to tie up. I bundle up all the important papers, everything that needs to be settled and leave it on my pillow. The thick manila envelope contains my will, freshly notarized and witnessed, as well a full confession. It's all in there, everything I've done, every bloody detail. I'd love to be able to see the headlines when it hits the press.

I spend my day making sure everything is ready. My knife is honed to a razor edge, my .38 is cleaned, oiled and working perfectly. I pack as much extra ammo as I can; I have no idea what's going to be waiting for me but I'm sure as hell not going to run out of bullets. I put on my best suit, and cinch up my favorite tie, the one I was wearing the day Gina told me she was pregnant. I take one last look around the rundown apartment that has been my home though this whole misadventure before I lock the door for the last time. The wind has died down, and the snow has stopped falling, through very little sun is cutting through the gray wall that hovers over my city. It'd have been nice to have seen the sun.

I drive across town to the boarded up wreck of McBride's Gym. It tears me up to see what's left of it. Boards cover the ruins of the doors, and the windows broken by gunfire. I know it's even worse inside and I can't stand the thought of seeing it like that again. I've made some arrangements, and it will thrive again. McBride's will be a fitting tribute to a great man; it's the least I can do for Kelly. He will not be forgotten.

My next stop is a quick run by the local post office. I send a letter to the most recent address I have for Delilah. God only knows where that woman has gotten herself to, but I have to at least try and get this to her. I need to tell her how sorry I am. I hope she can forgive me.

There are just not enough hours in the day to track down

everyone I should see. The list is longer than my arm and the day is nearly gone, so I skip to the last item on my list and roll over to the Deuce of Clubs. The place is pretty much empty as the day shift at the docks and the Randall Autoworks have yet to call it a day. The only patrons are the poor old bastards with nowhere to be and no one to be with. I'm thankful for the quiet, I need to see Franklin.

"You early, and dressed mighty fine tonight." He says as he gives me the once over.

"Been a busy day and I have an important appointment to keep tonight. Got a minute?"

"Sho do, sho do. Martha you mind the bar fo' a spell so's we kin talk. C'mon Boss." Franklin limps across the sawdust covered floor and I follow. He leads me off to the far corner, away from the fixtures at the bar. "You wants another gig all you gots ta do is ask." He laughs in his baritone rumble and gives me a big smile.

"Not this time, I need a favor actually." I take a small envelope out of pocket and slide it across the table to Franklin. "There's a safe deposit box at the downtown branch of the First National Bank, the instructions, key and everything you need is in there. I already put your name on it. I want you to take that key, go down tomorrow morning and clean that box out. Everything inside is yours." Franklin gives me a sideways look, eyes squinting.

"No one never gave me nuthin' in my life, and I didn't ask for nuthin' neither. What you up to?" His thick accent makes What You sound more like whatchoo.

"Just trying to do right by a man who deserves it. I need get going here Franklin, sorry. Got that appointment to keep."

"How's about this boss, I'll holds on to this fo' you. You come on back tomorrow and we kin go takes care of it together." I hear the concern in his voice.

"Tomorrow's all booked up, Franklin. You best see to it yourself."

"Naw suh, I'll keep it safe fo' you. Next time you by we'll go on down." I nod and offer my hand. He takes it both his rough mitts and hangs on for a long second. "You don't go do nuthin' stupid, boss."

"Me? Never." I give him another nod and I'm out the door. It's nearly show time, and I don't want to keep Doyle waiting. The drive back across town is as smooth as I could hope for, the weather holds just long enough to let me park down the street from the address Fingers provided. It's not quite ten, and I've got one more thing to see too.

I take the gold chain from around my neck and drop the simple wedding band into my gloved hand. I hold it tightly for a moment before I pull off my left glove and slide the ring back on my finger. I can hear the bells of Saint Andrew's tolling out the hour, it's time. I pull on my glove, and step out of the car.

Don't worry Gina baby, I'll be home soon.

36. On a Pale Horse

The night is perfectly dark; the only light is the dim glow from the street lamps. The storefront looks deserted, but that means next to nothing. I know all too well how many hideouts and old speakeasies dot this burgh and I'm sure this is yet another. There are two ways to play this, quiet and dirty, or loud and messy. I decide on the latter, I'm not in the mood for sneaking around. The front door isn't locked, which is a good sign.

The old florist seems to be abandoned, dust is everywhere. Even in the near total darkness I can see prints through the filth made by snow covered shoes and I follow them back. A second door is located just the other side of the counter, and it's far too close to be leading to the alley. This door is dead-bolted and locked tight when I try the handle. I guess it's time for my dramatic entrance. I put my .38 up close to the deadbolt and fire, the lock blowing out in a spray of shrapnel. I throw my full weight at the door smashing it inward. The door stops abruptly, a shout of pain of pain and surprise coming from the other side.

I fire twice through the door and kick hard again; a large forms slumps over, two holes in his chest, a large caliber pistol in hand. Well, that woke the hornets' nest. There are lights on just ahead down the short corridor; I can make out part of a stage. The shouts of at least five men ring through the old speakeasy. Well, no time to waste.

I step out into the main floor of the joint and fire twice at the first shape I see move. When he doesn't go down I fire a third and sprint hard for the bar. Bullets whine around me, I feel one clip my arm, white hot fire streaks across my bicep. Ignore it, run! I dive over the bar as more round tear the wall apart. I swing out the cylinder, and dump the spent shells as I crawl to the far side of the bar, the wood exploding around me. I slam six new rounds home as fast as I'm able. The firing slows for a second as everyone reloads and a burst of fire tears into the bar. I scream bloody murder for a second and let out a painful gasp, swinging my injured arm against the wall, flinging as much blood as I can against the wall, then lay still.

"I got him! I got him!" One of the voices chimes in, frantic and excited

"Go check! We got you covered." Another voice, this one less frantic, must be the one in charge.

"Yeah, yeah okay, I know I got him!" through the ringing in my ears I can just barely make out footsteps coming my way. I lay face down and keep deathly still, knife in hand, breath held. I see a shoe come around the bar, and then another briefly passes through my view. The goon prods me once with the tip of his gun; he leans in close, real close.

"I got him, he ain't moving! There's blood all over…." He doesn't get to finish. I drive my blade home into his thigh until I feel it nick bone. He screams, loud, and the firing starts again. I shove him hard back the way he came. I watch as several bullets crash into him and he topples over, shot through the chest.

"Oh God! Nick! You shot Nick you fucking idiots!" the calm voice isn't so calm now.

Good. I'm up and over the bar in one motion; the three remaining men have taken cover amongst some upturned tables in the middle of the hall. I fire twice in the direction of Mr. Calm and am richly rewarded by his blue suit sprouting two neat holes near his breast pocket. He collapses backwards silently. The goons turn on me but I'm already on top of the first, shooting him point blank in the head and making a god awful mess. I spin him towards his follow gang member as two rounds slam into his back. I feel the impact in my arms, I'm damn lucky he's not using a .45 or this wouldn't do a lick of good. When I hear that wonderful click of an empty revolver I toss the dead thug aside and close on the final mobster.

He's trying desperately to load his spent revolver as I close, bullets falling through shaking fingers. He gives up and tries to pistol whip me across the face. I bring my knife up and dig the razor sharp tip into his arm, stopping his blow immediately. He shrieks and clutches at the arm but my blade is already free and leaves a thin line across his throat as I slash. His face goes white as the blood begins to pour. His knees give out and he drops into the spreading pool. Nothing else is moving. No sign of Doyle. I catch sight of a door marked "Office" near the back of the joint. The door is slightly ajar. That has to be it, nowhere else to run.

I reload as I go, kicking the door open and leveling my pistol at the office chair, swung to face the rear wall.

"Turn around Doyle, so I can shoot you in the face." He doesn't move. "Turn the hell around you coward, I want you to see it coming!" It's then I notice the blood by the feet of the chair behind the small desk. Cautiously I make my way across the room, pistol covering the head of the seated figure. I turn the chair slowly, it's not Doyle. Fingers McNeely sits, still as the grave, knife buried to the hilt in his chest. There's no need to check for a pulse. There's a note, jammed on the hilt of the blade. Pick up the phone, is all it says. As if on cue, the office phone rings. I snatch it up from the receiver.

"Well boyo, I knew it was too much to hope the lads had killed ya. Yer an ace, no doubt!"

"Doyle you bastard!" I'm about to lay into him when he shouts me down.

"Shhh shhh shh! Quiet there laddie buck, I've something here of yours!"

"What?" What the hell is he talking about?

"Say hello there lovely." There's only silence, which is broken by a loud, ringing slap. "I said say hello to yer friend, bitch!"

"Fuck you Doyle!" Oh no, Dee! He's got Dee! The sound of fist meeting jaw comes through the line.

"Yer one impolite bitch and a thief to boot!" I can hear Doyle's sick cackle.

"You let her go you sick little troll or I'll…"

"You'll what? Kill me? Yer already on tha' way to do just that boyo! I'll make you a deal, though. You hurry over here and come quiet like good lad and p'raps there'll be enough of her left to walk away. I'd hurry t'were I you. The warehouse at the end of 49th. Ya better be swift sonny Jim!" The last thing I hear is Danny Doyle's mad cackle before the line goes dead.

37. End of the Line

This is the worst plan I've ever had, but I'm out of time and out of ideas. I'm standing outside the last bastion of the Doyle Gang, and the Devil himself is waiting inside. The snow that had relented just a few short hours before it begins again, soft white flakes falling from the pitch black sky. It feels right that this should end as it began. The two of gorillas at the door point their Thompsons at me. Slowly, very slowly I reach into my coat and pull my .38, then drop it into the snow. I do the same with my knife, letting it fall next to the discarded pistol. I put my hands up, behind my head.

One of the two steps cautiously down, the stairs and retrieves both my gun and knife with a feral grin. He sticks the barrel of the Thompson in the middle of my back and shoves me hard towards the stairway. I stumble a few steps but manage to keep my feet. He prods me on, up the rickety steps. The second thug opens the door and "helps" me through. I keep my hands on the back of my head as they march me down the darkened hallway, the only illumination coming from the open doors before and behind us.

We draw nearer to the end of the line, and I'm preparing myself for the worst. They shove me out into the light, the first thing I see is Danny Doyle, and the second is Delilah. She looks pretty bad; Danny worked her over pretty hard. One of her eyes is swollen shut; her cheeks are dark and bruised, there's a large cut on her forehead. She sags forwards against the ropes that bind her to the chair in the center of the large, open room. Her eye opens as the guards force me further into the room. She fixes her beautiful emerald orb on me for just a moment before it begins to water. I just give her a smile. She begins to sob.

"I don't think yer bitch is too happy to see ya! That's a shame, I was hopin' for a touchin' reunion!" Danny's voice is like nails on a chalkboard to me. It grates and grinds into my skulls until all I can think about is making it stop.

"She's not my bitch." The thug who retrieved my gear hustles across the room and hands both items to Danny. He smiles that predator's smile, teeth impossibly white.

"Hard ta' believe ya causes so much havoc with this relic! The knife though," he presses the release and the blade springs free. Danny jabs and slashes at the air a few times. "This is pretty nice. Think I'll keep it for me'self!"

"It's Italian, handmade."

"Fancy!" He releases the safety and collapses the blade, shoving it into his pocket.

"Ok, I'm here, you win. Let Delilah go."

"Ya, didn't really expect me ta' just let her wander off did ya? There's still a matter of ten thousand of me dollars she helped herself to!" He still got the predator's smile; he knows he's won, finally won.

"No Danny, I really didn't." Danny and his last two thugs laugh.

"Boys, start shootin' an' don't stop till yer empty! I made the mistake a' only shootin' him once last time!"

"Danny."

"Ah, time fer your famous last words is it?"

"You made another mistake." I dig my hands out of my sleeves and along come the twin .45's Delilah sent me so many months ago. I get a shot off at each thug, catching one between the eyes, and taking the other high in the chest. I never was a terribly good shot left handed. They both tumble backwards, one of the Thompsons squeezing off a stream of bullets that shatters windows and splinters wood. Danny points my .38 at me and pulls the trigger.

He's greeted by an empty click; he pulls again and again as I make way across the room to him. I point a .45 at his good leg, when I pull the trigger, it doesn't click.

Danny shrieks like a banshee as the .45 slug tears into his knee, shattering bone and leaving his knee a bloody ruin. He screams and he thrashes, clutching the wounded leg. I stomp down hard on his leg, and she shrieks again. I grab him by the lapel and look him dead in the face. His eyes are wild with pain and fear and impotent rage. I know that look well.

"Now you know how it feels." I kick the gun away from him and begin untying Delilah. She hasn't stopped sobbing. "It's ok D, you're safe now." She looks up at me, battered and bruised.

"I thought you hated the guns."

"Just saving them for a special occasion. Can you walk?" She nods her head weakly. I move around in front of her and take her hands gently. I'm about to pull her up when something explodes out my abdomen. It takes me half a second of awed shock to realize I've been impaled. The pain rips through me; it's not at all like getting shot. I slump to my side, tearing the blade out of Danny's blood slicked hand. The bastard had a sword cane, of course.

I hear a shot go off, distant and echoing. I see Delilah with one of the nickel plated .45s in her hands. It's the last thing I see before the world goes black.

I'm coming home, Gina. Sorry I was gone so long…

38. Saying Goodbye

There's a little cemetery just outside of town on a gentle hill that looks down on the city and the sea. It's a beautifully serene place, brick and wrought iron fences surround skeletal trees all layered in white. The last time I walked through those gates was to pay my respects to dear old Kelly, God rest his soul and lovely Delilah nearly got us both killed. I'm not so worried about that now. Ah, speak of the devil, there she is now.

Delilah makes her way through the gates and into the silence of the cemetery. The air is cold and still, but the snow has relented, at least for now. She's walking gingerly through the snow; poor thing isn't quite back together yet. She looks okay on the outside; the bruises on her face are mostly healed, but she still wears her long gloves more to cover the damage to her wrists than as proof against the cold. She's got a big bundle of roses, the crimson red contrasting with the stark whiteness of the world and impenetrable black of her outfit. Those beautiful green eyes are wet, poor girl has been crying again. There's been a lot of that lately. Her body is healing up fine; I'm not sure about the rest of her.

She makes her way slowly and carefully to the back of cemetery, moving with caution so as not to slip in the thin layer of snow and ice coating the stone path. It's not long before she stops, and carefully kneels down in the snow. She clings to the roses tightly while clearing the snow off the headstone. When the snow is finally clear she lays the bouquet beneath the name engraved on the bronze plaque, Kevin Sullivan. It's not long before the waterworks begin again. She tries to stand and get herself under control but it's a losing fight. She kneels and sobs and it breaks my heart all over again.

"You ought to be careful; you're going to have icicles hanging off your face in another minute or two." I make my way over to her side, and lean over her looking down at the headstone. "Kevin Sullivan? Which one was he?" She makes a big show of dabbing at her eyes with a handkerchief.

"He was my first husband and he was a kind and gentle soul! Not like you at all." she wipes at her face softly, not accomplishing much more than smearing her running mascara. "Today would have been our anniversary."

"Well, if you'd stop running husbands into the grave you wouldn't have to miss them so much." I step back out of her reach as quickly as my torn up insides let me.

"You help me up so I can slap you in the face!" I move over to her and offer my free hand "And for God's sake get rid of that horrid thing!"

"What this? This is a trophy, earned in battle and paid for in blood." The cane I'm leaning on is Doyle's, or more accurately, was Doyle's. It's not a bad piece of work, lacquered black, with a silver knob on top. You can barely see the seam where it pulls apart. I sure as hell didn't. All that elegance hides a deadly blade, a foot a half long. I can definitely speak to its effectiveness. From what I was told when I awoke, I had died on the operating table, for nearly two full minutes I was clinically deceased. One of the few things The War gave to Millburgh was a surplus of expertly trained trauma surgeons and they managed to bring me back. "I need a cane for now, why not this one?" We both groan as I help her to her feet. I haven't been out of the hospital long and it still feels like my insides are full of sharpened rocks. True to her word she slaps me in the face, but not like she means it, which is a nice change.

"That's absolutely ghoulish! Besides, why should you get the trophy? I killed him, and you're welcome very much. You're lucky I came back. I don't know how you'd get by without me." I take her arm; we make quite the pair, hobbling down the slick path.

"You realize that was five, right?"

"That doesn't count!"

We make our way out of the cemetery and back into the world of the living. The sounds of the day begin to filter in, the city waking from her cold slumber. The long winter isn't over, but for the first time in a very long while, I think I can begin to feel the spring.

www.ingramcontent.com/pod-product-compliance
Lightning Source LLC
Chambersburg PA
CBHW060620130626
46555CB00002B/595